THE
COFFIN
TREE

Asian Voices

THE COFFIN TREE

a novel by

Wendy Law-Yone

Beacon Press   Boston

Beacon Press
25 Beacon Street
Boston, Massachusetts 02108

Beacon Press books
are published under the auspices of
the Unitarian Universalist Association of Congregations.

Cover illustration: Balthus, Les joueurs de cartes (1968–73), Museum
Boymans-van Beuningen, Rotterdam.

94 93 92 91 90 89 88 87   8 7 6 5 4 3 2 1

Library of Congress Cataloging-in-Publication Data

Law-Yone, Wendy.
  The coffin tree.

  I. Title.
PS3562.A862C6 1987   813'.54   87–42848
ISBN 0–8070–8301–1

THIS BOOK IS DEDICATED TO CHUCK,
TO MY MOTHER AND FATHER,
AND TO THE MEMORY OF ALBAN.

PART ONE

1

Living things prefer to go on living.

When I was a child in monsoon country, this simple truth had yet to be revealed to me, so that in Grandmother's last invalid years I wondered what magic substance held her together. Was it the build-up of glue from all that starchy rice water she slurped up and swore by? Whatever it was, it kept her puny frame intact, year after year, stroke after crippling stroke. But when the last irreversible blow had landed, when she must have felt if not in her bones at least in the small bitter pit of her heart that her body was beyond repair, what was there to keep her hanging on except that blind purpose of all living organisms: to go on living?

She clung on for three full years. Her body was a shrunken vegetable; but strong roots had taken hold in her indestructible head. You could see them on the sides of her forehead—a network of blue-green veins beating angrily away.

She died one morning while I was at school. By the time I got home she'd been sponged and changed and was cool to the touch. Touching her was a struggle; but there they were, the servants, the relatives, the first of the mourners, watching me, hanging around like gawkers at a traffic accident.

I felt something like stage fright as I stood over her bed —weak knees, dry lips, and all. At last I touched her arm. It was stiff and shriveled and dry—the bark of an old tree. Not wanting to withdraw my hand too quickly, I slipped my fingers under her wrist. How light it was. She was never a large woman. On the contrary, she was smaller-boned than she appeared to be. But the illness had brought on some unaccountable weight. Here was a mystery: this desiccated little woman had become so leaden with paralysis that whenever she had to be shifted from bed to sofa, from sofa to deck chair, and back to bed—to ease her attacks of discomfort or boredom—it took two strong adults, huffing like furniture movers, to do the job.

All that weight was gone now. I could have picked her up single-handed. I thought of touching her forehead, but feared she might take it as a gesture of disrespect and fly into one of her rages, which were powerful enough, God forbid, to wake the dead.

She had a smile on her face. Not a pleasant smile: more a grimace suggesting an unsuccessful prank, as if, according to the old superstition, she had been making a face when the clock struck and froze that idiot expression for all time. Her head, shaven regularly at her request, now sprouted a stubble of gray that capped an old woman's untidy face, full of wrinkles and moles. She looked like a villainous acolyte.

The mourning adults were quick to give me the details: how they had turned her from side to side in order to swab the rubber sheet underneath her, how the bedsores festered, how the rubber stank from the urine and sweat and rotting flesh. I was fourteen at the time—old enough, apparently, to face the facts of death.

It seemed Grandmother knew when the end was near and turned her face to the wall, wailing, "But I am not well yet!" as though death could be begged off on grounds of poor health. She began to shake. They thought at first she was sobbing, but something funny evidently had struck her, causing spasms of helpless, tearful laughter. She died from the unbearable hilarity of her private joke.

Late that night, alone in my room, I found myself laughing, too. It wasn't that I'd thought of something funny; it was more like a sudden nervous tic. The next thing I knew, Grandmother was beside my bed. I saw her dark red velvet slippers—chicken-blood red, she used to call them—and looked up. Her hair glistened with coconut oil and smelled like macaroons. It was pulled back from her face and coiled tight around an ivory comb in a topknot that sat like a black stone on her head. I couldn't tell about her clothes, except that they hung loosely on her and reeked of mothballs and joss sticks.

She just stood there, casting a still shadow over me, with a look of stern puzzlement that came through even in the dark. I knew I had to stop laughing, but couldn't control myself at first.

"Why are you laughing?" Her interest in me was ominous.

"It's nothing, Grandmother." I began to tremble. "No reason. I'm just happy," I added foolishly, "that's all."

"Happy?" She let out a long, false laugh. "Happy! You're happy because I'm dead. You've been waiting for me to die. Witch!"

"Yes, Grandmother. No, Grandmother." In my fear I was willing to concede anything.

"Be happy, be happy!" she sang, and collapsed into a jerky, stylized dance, throwing up her arms, kicking up her heels, swirling round and round like a puppet in the hands of a crazed puppeteer. Where had she learned to dance like that?

The dance came to an abrupt end, in mid-step. She held the exaggerated pose and sang in falsetto: "Now. Tell: Happy you killed your mother? Happy she died giving birth to you? Happy now, little mother killer?"

Then she was gone, shuffling off in her thick velvet slippers. I could hear them dragging down the hall.

Her ghost prowled the house for months. Even though they had buried her, scoured her room, aired out the mildewed rugs and blankets, thrown open the windows to let in the sunshine she had hated; even after the servants had dusted and cleared the shelves of the home remedies she had clung to, I could still smell her. It was a smell of vanity and sickness, of aged sandalwood and obscure chemicals.

Long after she was bedridden, she had still insisted on plastering her face with sandalwood paste. Too sick to grind the paste herself, she would direct the maid from her bed. The maid sat on the floor, cushioned by her calves, hunched over the cosmetic stone which she rubbed with a chunk of sandalwood bark. She would rub and rub, breaking the hypnotic, circular motion only to sprinkle a handful of water now and then onto the stone, to correct the thickening paste. When the muddy, mustard-colored cream spilled over into the shallow trough cut around the stone dish, she would dip a finger into the mixture and offer it to Grandmother for inspection.

"No good," the old woman would pronounce. The paste was too thin or too thick for her liking. "Keep grinding, simpleton!" And the maid would grind away until, with luck, the old tyrant would fall asleep and the paste could be scraped hurriedly into one of her countless glass jars. Grandmother hoarded these vials in dark drawers and on hidden shelves, along with bundles of worn sandalwood stubs. After she died, I opened one of the sealed bottles. The paste had hardened like dried mud, and smelled of manure.

Her ghost carried not just her smells but her peculiar noises as well: the sluggish footsteps down the hallways; her groans as she lay on her stomach to be kneaded, slapped, and pounded upon by the blind masseur; her loud, lingering sighs.

My aunts, looking charred and withered in their black mourning clothes, still talked in whispers when they spoke of her, fearful of being overheard. Sometimes her shadow lurked in her old observation posts where, in her better days, she had kept suspicious vigil over our comings and goings.

Even now, when we sat down to meals, we half expected her to emerge from her room, flaunting her enamel chamber pot with arms outstretched, as if it were some ancient royal insignia. It wouldn't have surprised us to see her inching her way with regal abstraction across the room, past the dining table, and toward the bathroom, where the sound of her emptying the chamber pot and flushing the toilet would captivate us at the table. Then, just as we dared to begin the meal, she would have reappeared, chamber pot in hand, seething with silent reproach.

Months after her death, we felt she might at any moment pad out of her room in her odd, stiff shuffle and settle into position in the hallway to begin her old complaint: "Almighty God, I am so tired . . . losing blood . . . yes, losing blood. I feel it draining away, drying up in this hot air . . . can't eat anything, chest tight, stomach on fire. I've told the cook . . . fool!" (she would shout suddenly in the direction of the kitchen). "I've told you, how many times now? to cook the oil out of the curry!"

"He won't listen," (to herself) "thinks I don't know anything. No one listens to me. They all think they know so much, think reading and writing is everything. Look at me, what do I need to read and write for? To fry my brains? Did I need to read and write to find a husband? He liked me for myself. A good man. Inspector of police, a respected official. A good son, too. Looked up to his elders. Not like some people these days . . . "

Working herself up, she would let out a yell finally that shook the house. "Listen to me, dogs, pigs, animals! I was an important woman once, what do you know?!"

I still see her now, quivering with ineffectual violence, charging off into her room to fetch her trophy, her proof of power once enjoyed: a scratched and dented biscuit tin. She comes toward me (everyone else has had the good sense to look away, but I am riveted to her rage) and shakes the old box with its faded Chinese willow design in my face.

"My husband imported biscuits for me. They came in a tin like this. You think everyone could afford it? I was cared for, I tell you. A police inspector's wife. It broke his heart to leave me. His mother was ill; she lived in the West Country. I understood. He was a good son; that's what sons are for.

"But he was heartbroken, do you hear me? Heartbroken! Didn't he send me money? Didn't he long to see his daughter? The daughter I bore in this very womb?" (Dropping the tin onto the floor, she sticks out her stomach and beats on its flabby surface—an unresounding drum.) "But he never even saw his own daughter!" (voice breaking). "He couldn't come back, he had a sick mother to care for.

"If only he had seen his daughter! Beautiful? Hah! Never could *you* imagine such beauty. Skin as clear as tea. Hair like rope, but soft, soft—silk rope, not jute rope. My daughter, my only daughter!" (weeping now) "to die so young . . . to beget this . . . this . . . " (glaring at me, chuckling through her tears). "Look at you, just look at you," she says, laughing, crying. Then, overcome, she stands with her legs apart and drizzles a stream of urine onto the floor (the teak-wood floor which the servants have to get down on all fours and rub for hours with coconut husks to bring to that shine).

"Why are you looking at me?" Shrieking, she pins me to the wall with her glare.

"I'm not looking, Grandmother." But I'm unable to take my eyes off her, until she breaks the spell with a blinding, deafening cry of rage. "Out of my sight! Out! Out! The devil's in your eyes!"

The rain was loud and fierce the night Grandmother died. Early the next morning I lay in bed and listened to the drainpipes still dripping. The bread man bicycled in as usual, splashing through the puddles and rattling his bread box. I heard the familiar, petulant squeak of his brakes outside the servants' quarters.

Someone was singing: it was Shan coming home with another one of his annoying calypsos.

> When I was a lad jes three foot three
> Sartin questions occurred to me
> So I asked me father quite seriously . . .

Calypsos were a recent import: Harry Belafonte had passed through on a U.S. government cultural tour, and had sung at Town Hall. Shan had perfected the husky Belafonte tenor, but the calypsos got on my nerves. At school, any lapse into pidgin was punishable by one hundred corrective lines in the King's English.

"Not *me* father, *my* father," I'd interrupt him; but he would just sing on, grinning at my pedantry.

I hadn't seen him in days. I ran outside, ghoulishly eager to give him the news. He was walking up the long driveway to the house, singing into the wind:

So I asked me father quite seriously
To tell me de story bout de birds and de bees.
He stammered and he stuttered pathetically.
And this is what he said to me . . .

If I remember correctly his uniform of those days, he was in blue jeans and the old World War II jerkin that gave off goat smells. As on so many other mornings when he came home to catch up on sleep, his hair would have been uncombed, matted into curls by the humid air; his face unwashed and oily.

But he was in high spirits that morning. I could tell by his singing.

He had his sidekick in tow: a Chinatown cardsharp by the name of Billy Wing Ong. Billy was the poker king of the Chinese quarter—or so Shan would have me believe. Shan's friends weren't allowed to be ordinary. They needed stature—some quality to set them apart from the peons of the world—and he invented it for them. Billy the Poker King was nothing but a wastrel, filling his days with odd jobs and his nights with gambling; but as Shan's satellite, he had a certain notoriety to maintain.

Shan lifted me up and swung me around, playfully threatening to throw me over the angelica hedge, then setting me down only to begin his boxer's dance around me, tapping my face with light jabs and rabbit punches.

"Stop it," I said. "Listen to me. Grandmother's dead."

He let out a noise—an angry noise that seemed directed at me—then turned away and lowered himself, as an old sick man might, onto the stone bench at the foot of the lawn.

Billy was twitching with discomfort. He began to poke his foot in the dirt. I thought of the saying: *Dust does not rise when a dog flea hops.* He kept glancing up at Shan out of the corners of his eyes, which seemed, like a bug's, never to blink.

Shan said without looking up, "Go home, Wing Ong; I'll see you tomorrow."

Billy bit his lip and slunk away, a faithful dog cast out by a temperamental master.

Shan sat with his hands shielding his face but his mouth was uncovered, and trembling. "Poor old lady; poor, poor old lady."

It wasn't the first time I had seen him cry. He was ten years older than I, but closer to childhood in many ways. He cried easily—from anger, nostalgia, sometimes over a song. This unsettled me always: I envied his sensitivity but disapproved of it. Now I felt betrayed. A tyrant had died, setting us free. Why the sorrow?

"Don't cry," I said, without warmth. I could feel nothing but the grass sweating under my bare feet as I sat there in the early morning sun, unable to comfort my brother whom alone I cherished in a world of disheartening adults.

With Grandmother gone, my uncle and aunts, who would have been justified in joining hands and dancing over their freedom, were instead more subdued than ever. Uncle succumbed to inertia. He had a family of his own which he kept upcountry, but he himself preferred to stay with us, away from responsibility. Months would pass before his wife would pack up the children and board the train for the trip down south, to return Uncle to captivity.

Meanwhile, he impersonated a man free to be profoundly, voluptuously lazy. He spent his days reclining on a couch in one of the sitting rooms, an elbow under his head, a pillow cradling his soft paunch, lost in reverie. He had found his position and was loath to abandon it except to nourish or relieve himself or to relight his cheroot, and then he would leave behind a fine powder of ashes and skin peelings. The servants called him Old Snakeskin behind his back. Blowing smoke rings into the air, he picked away at the skin on his elbows, hands, and feet, inspecting each piece of tissue before flicking it over his shoulder absentmindedly.

Yet he was fastidious in his way. While my aunts ate with their fingers, he insisted always on silverware. With his fork he harpooned pieces of meat and vegetable straight out of the serving dishes, while his spoon paddled through the rice on his plate, folding in a touch of pepper paste here, a dollop of sauce there. The machinery never stopped: he mixed, chewed, and replenished his food with speed and efficiency absent from the rest of his life.

His meals were full of little noises: the crackle of raw vegetables and chicken bones between his teeth; the clucking and hissing when he bit into a "white-man's-poison" pepper; the *ting-ting-ting* as he played the spoon and fork.

My aunts would have been lost without those meals to supervise. Auntie Lily and Auntie Rosie were Mother's older cousins who had lived with us since she died. They were already in their sixties when I was in my teens, but ignorance kept them youthful. They chose to remain ignorant about things that happened *elsewhere*, that didn't directly concern knitting, shopping, or spying on the servants. Untroubled by the enormity of all that they didn't know, my aunts, despite their white hair and many missing teeth, remained girlish.

They were two years apart, but liked to dress alike and be mistaken for twins, although Lily was short, dusky, and thick through the middle, and Rosie was tall, fair, and shaped like a pear. Their Georgette blouses were frayed but crisp with starch; their fine silks were faded and thinning but still holding up; their hair was thinning, too, but there was enough left to wrap around jeweled combs. There was enough left, all in all, to flirt with the male masseur who came twice a week, and after he left to discuss celibacy as though the alternative were still an issue. For sex, as the saying went, "comes to an end only when one can no longer carry a handful of chaff."

But what my aunts did best was to wait on people at the dining table. They waited on Father, when he was home—sitting respectfully behind him as he hurried through his meal. They waited on Uncle, whose meals occupied the better part of their days. They waited, working their eyebrows disapprovingly, on Shan and his shady friends. And of course they waited on me.

They fretted over my appetite daily.

"See this rice? So fluffy and white! Take a little more, child, and a small spoonful of meat. Meat is strengthening. All right, then, leave the meat, but try one or two of these long-stemmed mushrooms, they'll melt in your mouth, the cook made them just for you."

When my aunts were occupied, one of the servants would coax me through the meal. The cook's wife, a fat woman with a cluster of raisiny moles where ear met cheek and the temperament of a high-strung cat, had the habit of standing over the table and waving a large nipa fan while I ate.

"Why do you do that?" I asked her one day.

"Do what, child?"

"Fan me like that?"

"To make you feel good."

"But it doesn't. It only makes the food cold."

"Hot, cold, what does it matter?" She banged the fan down on the table, embarrassed.

"You don't eat anyway," she said, her voice rising. "Take a look at yourself: all skin and bone. You'll go off someday to meet your lover in the dark—if you're lucky, hah—and he won't know whether you're coming or going."

I joined in the laughter that came from the kitchen. But back in my room I locked the door and leaned into the mirror, pressing my hot forehead against the cool glass. Nose to nose with myself, the familiar self-loathing began.

Portraits and heavily touched-up photographs of my

mother hung throughout the house. They showed a young woman of arresting delicacy: long-limbed, long-fingered, slight as a dancer. Her hair, black and thick, was peaked at the brow and framed her face like a low, neat cap. Her wide, moist eyes had the look of a startled doe.

All that perfection had been squandered to produce my lusterless hair; my square-tipped fingers with the unsightly, bitten-off nails; my dark skin, broad face, and the half-moon shadows under my eyes that branded me with an old woman's look.

What right had I, then, to take offense at reminders of my plainness? In the uneven, precarious rhythms of my heart, I felt that the only safe refuge was reason. So, clinging to reason and manners, I could join the laughter at my expense, keeping the stings and burns under wraps.

But I was never innocent. I knew it was unnatural to deny those adults my anger and tears, that it made them wonder and at heart uneasy.

The monsoons, always long, seemed endless that year. Rain dinned on the rooftops day after day, and the heavy wet winds tore branches off the banyan trees. I stayed indoors sometimes for ten days at a time, staring out the windows at the thin papaya trees aslant in the rain, at the water's edge down at the foot of the rolling lawn. The lake swelled up to lick the railings of the derelict gazebo where bullfrogs and lizards took shelter, nodding sociably, then hopping and darting back out into the rain.

One afternoon, during a lull, Shan and I went down to the lake where the old raft we had built out of a hardwood packing crate was moored to the starfruit tree. The shouting rain had let up briefly. We sat on the raft, idly plucking at the white water hyacinths that had sprung up between the cracks, while a carp, stranded in the mud, seemed to watch us with ancient, lifeless eyes.

On an impulse, we untied the raft and pushed off, out through the hyacinth-choked inlet into the open lake. Shan had fetched the pair of sampan oars that lay unused and rotting behind the gazebo and, taking one apiece, we paddled along the bank through a tunnel of willows that brushed the water, until we came to a small orchard we had never noticed before.

The trees bore an unfamiliar fruit—thick-skinned like mangosteens, but fuzzy and flesh-colored. The branches drooped from the weight of hundreds of these little round heads, hanging by calyxes that looked like flowered hats. We knocked the fruit down with sticks and were hurrying back to the raft with our hands full when the orchard keeper, a skeletal old man with collapsed cheeks and a gaping black hole for a mouth, hobbled out of the bushes.

"Wicked little thieves," he whined, and came after us with a stick.

We bounded into the lake, dropping fruit left and right and splashing the old man until his loincloth was soaked. We leaped onto the raft and pushed home, looking back from a safe distance.

He was standing knee-deep in water, his small, bony pelvis thrust forward. With one hand he had drawn his loincloth aside, and in the other he was bouncing his insignificant little cluster of genitals.

"Look, look!" he called after us. "I'm an old man, too old to catch you. But I'm a man!" He began to giggle.

We drifted along in silence.

"Terrible to be old," Shan said at last.

"I'll never be," I said.

"Oh? What will you do? Drink potions? Find the magic onion that will keep you young?"

"I'll kill myself when I'm old and useless."

He spat into the lake—a reflex of superstition.

"Don't talk like that," he said. "You know it's bad luck."

"Life is bad luck. Being born is bad luck."

"Someday," he said, "you'll grow up and be thankful for what you have."

"What's that?"

He was used to my constant pleas for reassurance, but was unstinting each time.

"You are healthy and strong, and very, very smart," he said, repeating a phrase I would never tire of hearing. "Also, you are my sister; I'll look after you."

We are allies, after all!

I reached down to touch the water and came up with a handful of liquid sunlight. In that moment when the waters of the polluted lake sparkled like a tawny amethyst in my hand, the world with all its risks and dangers seemed to shrink a little, into something almost manageable.

2

When Father was in his twenties, he left home without a word to his parents and joined the Revolution of the Hill-tribes. He had been raised in the south, in the capital city of Rangoon, where his father had made his fortune. It was around the turn of the century that Grandfather, who had served as economic adviser to the king, and minister of forestry and agriculture after the monarchy was ousted, became an entrepreneur. He cornered those markets once within his portfolio—teak, rubber, rice, tea—and went on to buy up fisheries, jade mines, race tracks, distilleries.

In his old age he worried about his spiritual future and atoned for his wealth by accumulating merits for the here-after. He patronized monasteries, commissioned the building of pagodas, and gave to charities money that might have gone, under normal circumstances, to his only son.

But Father had renounced his legacy while still a student at the university. In his first year he fell in with radicals from the dissident minorities who lured him away (as Grandfather needed to believe) to a rebel stronghold in the border region of the northeast. There he joined the Hill States' fight for secession from the lowland government. Ten years would pass before Father returned home. By then Grandfather had died, leaving his wealth to everyone, it seemed, except his renegade son. To him Grandfather had bequeathed one small piece of his vast residential properties: the spacious timber-and-brick house in which I grew up.

In Father's second year as a revolutionary he took up with a woman from one of the rebel villages. She must have been prettier than average, or very young at any rate—fifteen or sixteen at most. By twenty the women of her tribe were already showing rotting teeth and breasts that sagged to their waists. From what I had seen of such women in the village bazaars up north, I supposed her to have short legs, smooth skin, a blush on her high-boned cheeks, and narrow, hooded eyes.

When I had reached that point in adolescent consciousness of imagining my father's sexuality, the image of this hilltribe girl sprang to mind more readily than that of my mother, his second (and official) wife. Yet what my inchoate fantasies led to were not so much details of seduction and consummation, but the clearer, starker imagery of my father's impatience. I imagined him frantic to tear off the girl's coarse, cumbersome tunic, her long sash of melon seeds that would round the slope of her hips.

I knew only too well how he behaved in heat, albeit of a different element. At home, fear of this heat reduced us to mere subjects before a capricious god. His impatience alone could inflict damage on the order of a natural disaster.

I am thinking now of the period following the early insurrections, when the People's Army he built had won its first war against the central government, and he had seized the power he seemed born to wield. (This was when I was about eleven or twelve.)

He would come home without warning at irregular hours, and at the sound of his limousine rolling up the gravel driveway, the household snapped to attention. *Would it please the general to dine now? Would the general care for a drink? A massage?* The servants bowed and squirmed, ducked their heads and lowered their eyes as they awaited orders. To my knowledge he never actually chastised any of them, but instinct told them never to put him to the test. His potential for violence was as explicit as that of the fire-breathing dragon tattooed so graphically, in blue and green, on his left forearm.

Once, reaching for a box of cigarettes (the 555 brand he smoked came in flat metal boxes in those days), he found it packed instead with tiny multicolored buttons, turned into a sewing box by an unwitting maid. Because he demanded the efficiency of things in their designated places (cigarettes —not buttons—in cigarette boxes) and because some soft-headed servant had played, however unintentionally, a practical joke on him, he took the offending box and flung it against the wall.

Confetti-colored buttons showered the room in a sudden mirage of festivity.

I was on my knees in an instant, cowed into servitude by fear and shame. I scurried around the floor, scooping up buttons by the handful. As I hastened to remove all traces of his tantrum before anyone else walked in, I could see out of the sides of my eyes my father the general's heavy khaki boots, thick-soled, mud-streaked, and standing uncannily still.

I picked up as many buttons as I could without going too close to his feet. My eyes never ventured above the level of his knees. Pretending to be absorbed in my task, I moved away from him, closer and closer to the door, and backed out of the room, still crawling.

Father's young woman was pregnant before long. Eight months later she went into labor during a terrible storm. It was one of those late-monsoon storms that began with a low rumbling and gurgling from the skies, as from the belly of some famished giant. The winds would whip through the bamboo huts and snatch off whole roofs of thatch. Under the crackle and clap of thunder, small children clutched their heads and kowtowed in fear, praying, *Save us, save us!* afraid that the lightning would set the sky on fire.

It was in such a storm that the woman delivered her firstborn. After the lightning and thunder and churning winds, when the sound of mountains crumbling and oceans roaring had died down and rain began to pelt the roof, she picked up an empty cane basket, held it like a shield against the hammering downpour, and walked straight out into the bamboo grove, past the spot where the men built wood fires at night. The men—the father of her child included—were away that night on a raid and would be gone from the village for what could be several more days.

In a small clearing she squatted over a banana leaf. The rain slashed down. Pain tore in and out of her body, lasting the length of the rainstorm.

When the rain began to let up at last, the small head broke through, was caught by the mother's hands, and pulled. Placing the small, limp body on the banana leaf, the woman fell forward on her knees, panting like an overworked beast of burden. A tide was turning in her womb again, heaving and swelling between her legs.

Lord God. Another head.

Afterwards, the mother of twins lay on the floor of her hut and the village women muttered, "Madwoman! Going out into the storm like that!" while an old crone sat in a corner and sang, *Doom, doom! Two is a bad omen. Never mind. The first was dead, thank the spirits. Pretend it's one child. Give it a strong name. And pray.*

What could be stronger than a mountain?

And so they named him Shan.

It was childbirth, the villagers said, that drove his mother wild; it was he, the bad-luck baby, the sickly runt, that robbed her of sleep and her mind. She would listen to his sticky breathing with its bubbly *khroo-khraw* sound of a haunted stream, and sniff the air with a jungle beast's attention to danger in the wind.

By the time Shan was a toddler—fast on his feet now, and no longer sickly—she was off and wandering through the hills. The village women tended and fed him like their own, even chewing his rice for him between their tobacco-blackened teeth, and packing into the child's open mouth the discolored lumps of paste.

His mother was seldom to be seen; but sometimes, he'd spot her in the distance, crisscrossing the pathways at a slight jog, swinging her arms raffishly.

Her people supposed the lunacy to be a curse—just one of a hundred that childbirth could carry. But suppose the wild weed of insanity had been creeping through the woman even as Father bedded her? Father wasn't one to be put off by the disordered psyche of some mountain woman, if he noticed the signs at all. He preferred to separate himself from any frailties of spirit or mind. They tended, like an amputated arm, a game leg, to slow things down.

I envied Shan his memories of a mother, dismal as they were. *This is how she looked in the dark.* Baring his teeth in a jackal's grin, he could work up a mouthful of spittle and froth at the mouth. *She came at me like this.* He showed me how she thrust out her hands like pitchforks, ready (to judge from the fire in her eyes) to rake him to shreds, but instead taking his head in her dirt-caked hands and shaking it with some sentiment akin to love.

Once, when he was twelve, he came home to the village from a morning of fishing and found his mother alone on the floor of the hut, sitting with her chin on one knee. She was recovering from some unfathomable grief, wracked with sobs and shudders. He stood uncertainly in the doorway, but when he approached her, saying, *Mother?* she stopped him with a scream.

"Like this," he said, turned his face away from me as though to cough, and let out a head-splitting cry, so savage and so strange that it made my skin crawl.

We had been sitting in the old Portuguese cemetery at the far end of the lake where we sometimes went prowling at night for the lurid enchantment of telling ghost stories and catching fireflies, which we made believe were the fugitive souls of the dead.

I felt the ground shift beneath my feet from that scream and wondered if the buried bodies had stirred in unison.

"Let's go home," I pleaded. I was overcome by the night, badly scared by everything around me: my half-brother with his dreadful memories, the dead underfoot, the flickering firefly souls. My muddy feet appeared in the moonlight to be cast in molten pewter and felt as heavy. Even the lake seemed bewitched as we bobbed home on the raft. I dropped the jar of dead fireflies into the lake and watched it catch the moonlight as it rode the black waters.

Along the banks, crickets were chirring; bullfrogs bellowed; lizards clucked and ticked. But it was one of those times in my childhood when it was hard to believe in the importance of the living.

My own mother came to me only in the slow suffocation of sleepless nights. I was no older than seven when I used to sleep blindfolded, a precaution against waking up wide-eyed in the dead of night to find some long-haired, long-tongued witch leering at the window of my room.

It was Shan who told me about witches and such.

Jogging through the empty city streets at dawn one day, he saw something move among the leaves of one of the jacaranda trees that lined the road. Thinking it might be a large tree squirrel, he stopped to peer up into the branches.

There, perched in the fork of a branch, was a woman with blood-red lips and black hair that hung down her back, tousled and free, like a harlot's.

She beckoned to Shan. He took a step forward. She bent down then, and uncoiled out of her mouth a tongue as long and smooth as a banded krait. The two-foot-long tongue shot out to give his mouth a quick cold lick with its slimy tip, and sent him running like the wind, rubbing his mouth all the way.

His stories kept me awake, with the cotton napkin burning into my eyes like a bread-and-onion poultice. Gradually, in the closed tent of my olive mosquito net, my mother would be revealed to me. The encounter always took place in her dressing room, where I'd find her seated in front of the carved gilt mirror, her back to the doorway where I stood and watched.

I could see her long, narrow back and neck, the shining coils of hair, and, in the mirror, the small shoulders and breasts, the startled doll-like face.

Pressed to the doorway it was my compulsion to ask, "Are you going out tonight?" And it was her habit to answer, as she rummaged in a drawer for some trinket to distract me with, "Yes, but Mama will be home soon."

Enthralled, I'd watch her sketch in the shallow geography of her face, penciling her eyebrows with small steady strokes, spreading pale pools of color across her cheeks, following the hillocks of her lips with a stick of shimmering cinnabar, and lastly, with rapid dabs of the powder puff, turning her skin into a dusty gold.

Afterwards, she would pull out the drawer of perfumes and reach into it for a thin spiral bottle, the sight of which filled me with panic that spread like heartburn from stomach to throat. She would unscrew the top, place her index finger over the opening, tilt the bottle over with a flick of her wrist, and touch the back of her ears, her neck, and the hollow between her breasts, with that single drop of perfume.

The scent washed over me then, a greenish fragrance that released a half-formed memory of sunlight and breeze and rain-soaked grass—a memory made all the more precious by the certainty of loss to follow. As though it attacked my tear ducts directly, the scent decanted a flow of stinging tears.

"Don't go," I begged, rushing at her, at once miserable and ashamed of my misery. "Please don't go." I clung to her with my thin dark arms like some scrawny simian.

In the end I had to be peeled away by firm hands, while I struggled and sobbed.

"Child, child, you're dreaming again," a voice would say —the voice of a servant or aunt. "What's to be afraid of? A houseful of people to look after you, and you act this way."

When I sank into sleep again, the mosquito net tucked firmly into the sides of my bed once more, it was with the glimpse of real promise, as if in the moment of drowning the shadow of a raft played on the water's surface. Mother had left; the ordeal of severance was over; now I could continue my vigil until her return.

But the vigil brought new dangers that came in strange forms—most often in the form of a centaur.

I could see, even through clenched eyes, the great hefty creature, so cunningly built that I couldn't tell where man ended and beast began.

The human half was bestial, sinewy and shining with

sweat, while something appallingly human was built into the horse flanks and legs. It watched me with unwholesome interest from the corners of its wide, erotic eyes, nostrils flaring, tossing its male head, horse-style, to taunt and tease me, while the hoofed legs stomped and paced with familiar human impatience, now rearing up over my bed, now prancing roguishly, finally thundering round and round in a murderous gallop that pinned me, sweating, to the side of my bed against the wall.

Mama! I'd call out in a voice so feeble I could barely hear myself. But she would appear over me, bending down with the gift of her voice and her body odor of freshly squeezed sugarcane juice.

"I'm so scared," I'd say in her ear.

"Scared! Of what? God is watching over you."

"The man and the horse," I would whisper, afraid to call it a monster or any other name that might incur its displeasure and spite.

But, waking, I thought: If God is watching, if He sees and lets such things happen, there is no telling what He might do next.

The God who had claimed me was not the same God who ruled over my family and friends. Mother had been a convert to Catholicism and for her sake I was sent to a school run by the Irish nuns. But I had my doubts all along.

I still have a snapshot of First Communion day—a scorched-looking print that retains the eggy smell of the chemical coating used in the old photo studios. It shows me at age seven, standing somber and furtive on a sidewalk outside the Church of St. Teresa, holding a white prayer book in both hands, and dwarfed by yards of white tulle. The veil is held down by a crown of fake flowers; the long dress trails in the dirt of the pavement.

My Buddhist friends, meanwhile, were going through

initiations enviably unlike mine. When we compared photographs at school, it pained me to see the contrast: They posed like princesses on gilded platforms, all spangle and flash in their silks and laces, in their rhinestone headdresses and sequined cardboard "wings." And their faces were painted!

"But it hurt like anything!" they would complain for my benefit—about the one little inconvenience of their coming-of-age ceremony, when the needle was passed through their earlobes. "You had it easier."

I knew they were only trying to console me for the drabness of my lot. With their new earrings that winked in the light, they could afford to be kind. I would gladly have endured the pinprick for the reward of those small diamond-studded nuts and gold bolts anchored to their ears.

The spoils of my own initiation were shabby by comparison: a string of garnet-colored rosary beads and a prayer book blessed by the Pope. The rosary broke easily and needed constant mending; the prayer book had no pictures and its glue smelled of spit. As for the Pope, the high priest who could make no mistake, he was not so marvelous as the fakirs and fire-eaters who danced like devils through the streets on Hindu holidays.

Inside the Church of St. Teresa, the priest leading us through our First Communion performed his own brand of black magic, heartily swirling the blood of Christ in the shiny goblet, downing it with relish, and wiping his stained lips with a crisp napkin, as after a robust meal. And there we were, the children of God, throwing our heads back and our tongues out to receive the flesh of our Father's son, transformed by some abracadabra into blank coins of bread.

The savagery sickened me. The bread attached itself to the back of my palate as I walked back down the aisle, dizzy from the fear that before I could reach my seat, in full view of the congregation, I would choke and spit up the host on the creamy marble floor.

In the years that followed I seldom left the Communion rail without a surge of nausea. It was part of the odious duty of having to devour the flesh and blood of a brutalized God whose suffering I was somehow responsible for. Faith was all mystery and teaser: a God with many masquerades, disguised now as dove, now as mistreated man, now as king; a God that spoke in riddles to be accepted, not solved; a God that dreamed us up, let us loose, sat back to watch our mistakes, then held them against us, knowing all the while that we never stood a chance.

For all the sermons and catechisms, I couldn't escape the confusion, the feeling of being stood on my head. If anything, the parables terrified without clarifying. I feared mortal sin not because of the offense to God, but because of a Redemptorist priest's allegory:

A man murdered a friend of his—out of anger, jealousy, greed, who knows? It doesn't matter. When he woke up the next day he almost fell over from fright. The corpse of his murdered friend had been chained to him. It was a heavy iron chain. Unbreakable. No key to it. No lock, even.

For days the murderer was forced to drag the body around with him throughout the house. To the bathroom. To the kitchen. To bed. He couldn't undo the chain himself, and he couldn't call for help, for then he would be exposing his crime.

Meanwhile, the body began to rot. It began to bubble up and fester. Then flies came in swarms. Maggots crawled in and out of its nose, its ears, its eyes. By and by the corpse was humming with dung beetles and orange crabs.

The murderer stayed chained to the body, because by then he was raving.

So, too, with mortal sin. It is a rotting corpse we drag around with us, until we confess and repent.

3

Chance had singled me out to side with a God who was foreign to my world, but whose power over me was unanswerable. It was not unlike Father's power. I could never have challenged him, either. Or counted his secrets.

He kept so much from us.

Take the day the tanks rolled into the streets and the trucks surrounded our house. He must have known in advance, because he had already fled when it happened. Yet he had told us nothing, so that my brother and I, in our ignorance, slept through it all—through the sharp knocks on the front door, through the absurdly polite exchange between the arresting officer and Auntie Lily.

Later, trembling at the recollection, she told us how it went:

"Excuse the disturbance, so early in the morning. Where is he?"

"He's not here." ("Should I have pretended whom they meant by *he*? No. They knew that I knew what they wanted.")

"Has he gone out, then?"

"Yes. He is gone a lot. We hardly see him."

"How long this time?"

"A week, maybe ten days. We never know."

"May we come in and look? We have our duty. Just a quick look. Is it allowed?"

"Officer! Would we dare stop you? Come. But quietly, please. The children are asleep."

(We were seventeen and twenty-seven by then, but still children to my aunts.)

They satisfied themselves in less than ten minutes of a desultory search. Then, at the front door, the officer turned to Auntie Lily and bowed. "We thank you, Auntie. Go get some sleep." He sounded almost affectionate.

Auntie! The familiarity would have been laughable, except in our society of bogus familial connections, where everyone was an aunt or an uncle, a brother or a sister—even as enemies.

All that day the planes droned overhead like giant mosquitoes in a bad dream. The tattoo of gunfire was as loud as a construction drill. Early the next morning, just when silence seemed to have been restored, the glass palace was strafed to smithereens and the old clock tower went haywire, clanging wildly, sounding its own alarm.

While the radio stations maintained their scratchy silence, the servants ventured outside and returned with their own bulletins and a new foreign word which they pronounced in twos, as if calling to the doves: *Coo! Coo!*

My aunts relayed the news to Uncle. "Cousin, it's true. Coo! Coo!"

Then Auntie Rosie thought to ask: "What's coo?"

"You don't know?" said Uncle.

"How should I know, Cousin? I'm telling you what I heard. Would I ask if I knew?"

Uncle was caught. "A coo, you ignorant girl, you know-nothing, is what's happening now."

"So, so, so. Like that. I understand now," said Rosie, lying.

Afterwards, in the kitchen, I heard her say, "Minnow, what does it mean? . . . Coo! Coo!"

Minnow was the cook, a delicate man. Some near-fatal disease of infancy had arrested his growth so that even in his thirties, he could have passed for a twelve-year-old boy. Tiny, moist-eyed, tormented by the other servants for having been to school, he burst into tears about once a month.

"Coup, mistress? Coup is when one government kicks out another government. Oh, mistress, I'm so afraid."

"Coward," said Lily, who had just come into the room. "Act like a man."

In her ignorance, it escaped her that this was bad advice. Prince R's son had acted like a man on the morning of the coup and left his mark—in bloodstains on his parents' imported marble portico. From his bedroom window, he had seen his father being prodded with machine guns into a van. Shouting, "Fight, Father, fight!" he had raced downstairs, clearing a whole flight of stairs with one jump, and got as far as the front door, where the blast of gunfire lifted him off the floor. They continued to pump holes into his body even after it had ceased twitching on the floor of Florentine *pietra morta*.

The prince's son was about my age. When news of his death reached us, I couldn't imagine dying as he had. This may have been because I couldn't imagine Father submitting to capture without a struggle. More likely, I knew my own cowardice.

I had seen that fear could stimulate courage, but it didn't

work that way for me. Instead it made me shrink. I shrank from the endless family discussions about the damages done by the coup: nationalization; demonetization; surveillance; censorship; curfews; confiscations; rations; midnight arrests. I shrank from puzzling out my father's disappearance, and simply accepted the secret, sovereign nature of his mission. I shrank from the contemplation of any protest: That was my father's business. I shrank from my own womanhood, binding my breasts with rolls of elastic bandage as cruelly and senselessly as the Chinese used to bind their baby girls' feet. And, though no one would believe me, I even shrank in height. Between the ages of eighteen and twenty, I shrank a full inch, but my aunts would insist that this was impossible: You can turn gray before your time, they used to say; but you can't shrink until you're old. Their ignorance persisted.

Little by little, I began to see some wisdom in my relatives' ways. Once I had thought of my aunts' lack of curiosity as a form of willful blindness undeserving of pity; now I became incurious myself. I could achieve this more easily since I was no longer in school (the coup had coincided with my last year of high school). And though I could not completely insulate myself from the epidemic of woes, I was protected by the kind of apathy induced by long war movies in which the excess of noise, violence, and death cauterizes the senses and makes it all meaningless.

People were disappearing in unexplained arrests. Banks, shops, offices were closing one by one. Schools were being run by uniformed men. Caught in a downtown riot, one of our neighbors was burned to death in a bonfire. The proprietor of a fabric store my aunts used to frequent shot himself on Demonetization Day. Chary of state banks, he had withdrawn his savings a week before and taken home the money in large bills, which he then cunningly sewed into the fibers of his hemp mattress. He left a note: "Where is hope when the mattress is worth more than the money it conceals?"

Yet none of these calamities weighed on me. They were disturbing—but roughly in the way that a whispered conversation can be disturbing when you are trying to fall asleep. What weighed on me were my own small physical ailments. In the summer, fearful of suffocating in the dust and heat, I was prone to gulping air, and kept to my room with the blinds drawn and the ceiling fan churning. In the rainy season, I ground my teeth at night from the aches in my bones; by day, obsessed by fungus and mold, I sniffed everything—food, clothing, furniture, books—for the signs of mildew. Feeling leached, I slept and slept until I couldn't tell whether I slept so much because I was run-down, or whether the reverse was true. Not only did I condone Uncle's lethargy, I surpassed it.

Uncle's own response to any kind of bad news was short and philosophical: *Must be*.

"Cousin," one of my aunts would say, "have you heard? What's his name, you know, your old boss's brother-in-law, the one whose uncle, the doctor, performed the operation on your wife's sister when she had the goiter? Gone. Arrested. So old. He'll never live through jail."

Uncle would nod, chomp on his cheroot with his long, rabbity teeth, and stare at a corner of the wall. Then, quietly, he'd say: "Yes. Must be."

Or: "Cousin, the rice is inedible. The cook wasn't watching. You'll have to wait another half hour. We'll cook a fresh pot. Agreed?"

And Uncle, after emitting one of his doleful, lowing belches: "Must be. Yes, must be."

Although I avoided the newspapers and the radio, there was no ignoring the spreading food shortages, the rumors of famine, the bankruptcies, the secret police. And with each new injustice, I, too, began to think: *Must be*.

This was the worse corrosion—this loss of courage, outrage, and will—and it was eating into the others as well. Our whole household was in jeopardy: Father's remittances came too irregularly to count on; my aunts were worried about bazaar money; the servants were worried about being let go; and, as dependents of a rebel leader still on the loose, none of us was safe. Yet we carried on submissively, accepting everything as if there were no alternative even to dream about or talk about and keeping down our voices and hopes.

In no time at all, oppression became the only reality, and life seemed meant to be lived underhandedly, with cat-and-mouse cunning. My aunts, once so incapable of guile, now threw themselves into daily intrigue, though they had neither the practice nor the flair. Auntie Lily telephoned a friend one day to report the small success of buying a pound of black market butter, and spelled out the word "butter" as if that were a cryptogram.

The strange truth was that my aunts were blossoming, not withering, in that airless atmosphere. The day brought new tasks, new challenges. Disputes among the servants were on the rise, and these had to be mediated and settled. Housekeeping was complicated by the shortage of one thing and another. Shopping was a matter of luck and pluck, being part lottery, part foray.

Every morning, returning home from the bazaar, Auntie Lily would complain of weakness, Auntie Rosie of thirst. But a pinch of snuff and a glass of water would revive them enough to report on the day's exertions.

"Ahlala, the lines!" Lily would say; and Rosie would add a hiss—not of derision but of confirmation.

"People standing since dawn for a can of condensed milk," Lily would go on.

"Ssshhheee . . . "

"Lucky we're old, no? At least people take pity and give us their places. May they live long."

"Ssshhheee . . . "

"I don't mind waiting; others have to wait. But enough of that open-air market!" (Here Lily bowed her head and waved goodbye to whatever it was she had had enough of.) "I knew something was up when the fellow selling us the combs began looking here and there and acting like a monkey that just cut its prick on a blade of grass. How do they know when the police are coming? How can they tell? A secret signal, I suppose. Next thing we knew, whistles were blowing, the police were everywhere, isn't it so, Sister? But those hawkers are magicians. You should have seen the way they just threw everything into boxes and bags and made like they were part of the crowd. The police took away a couple. The wife was crying; the husband was grinning like a fool—it had to be fear. But maybe they weren't husband and wife; maybe they were brother and sister; what do you think, Rosie?"

"Ssshhheee . . . "

"Anyway. The law can't stop those hawkers. It would be like digging a well on high ground. Five minutes after the police were gone—five minutes, imagine—they were at it again, putting out all their odds and ends. Not that anyone would look twice at these things in good times: empty whiskey bottles, broken fountain pens, car spare parts, dented pots and pans. But these days you have to look for a squirrel till you find a bird."

After these brushes with the black market, my aunts would join the lines at one of the People's Stores, with its air of a raffle or a lucky dip.

But when my aunts' turn came, the clerk at the counter would have little to offer.

If they said, "Salt, please?" he would invariably say, "Yes, Auntie. We have no salt."

"Oil?"

"Yes, we have none."

"Sugar. Give us some sugar, in that case."

"Sugar? Yes. No sugar."

"Aspirin, then."

"Yes. We don't have."

"Hè! Then what do you have?"

"Ointment, Auntie; ringworm ointment."

"What for? We are a bathing family, not a scabby one."

"Take it, dear Aunt. You never know."

On this occasion, Rosie, who never could pass up an opportunity for wordplay, would say, "There is the saying, don't you know? 'He who has ringworm fears no freckles.'" And then she would titter at her own boldness, and hang her head while Lily told her off: "What's with you? Don't be so long-of-tongue."

Once, my aunts went out to buy vinegar, jaggery, and some cotton thread—and came home instead with two pairs of men's undershorts, made in China and labeled: Double-Barrel Brand. They laughed over that little joke for days, Lily coughing and gagging between raspy chuckles, and Rosie shaking as she let out one long hiss of mirth.

They were taking it all with astonishing good humor. Even when they had to dip into their gems just to raise bazaar money, their regret seemed slight; in fact, they welcomed the furtive little transactions with the black market buyer who reeked of Tiger Balm and shook his right leg incessantly while poring over their tiny paper envelopes of loose rubies and sapphires, zircons and pearls, alexandrite and jade. He would take out an eyeglass (which bore an uncanny resemblance to the indigo-blue plastic cup that came with Optrex, an eyewash my aunts used) and peer at the glassy little stones, looking for flaws (or "sores" as they were called in the trade).

All the while, my aunts kept up their sales prattle and flirted with him as they poked through their jewels—Auntie

Lily with her short dark index finger, and Auntie Rosie with the rusty tweezers ordinarily used to pluck out her sparse wisps of underarm hair.

Adversity forced these two old ladies out into a world they had for so long ignored; and now, worldly-wise, in their newfound element, they no longer concerned themselves with the circumstances that had brought them there, but were content to work out the simple details of conniving and surviving.

But something was taking its toll on them—though whether it was the stresses of the times or just the aging process it was hard to tell. In the space of less than a year, my aunts had acquired some exaggerated traits. They were easily, too easily, startled these days: by the sudden bang of a door, the jingle of coin, the sizzle of oil, the rustle of a dry leaf. It didn't take much to set them off. They would jump, utter some little exclamation of fright, and beat their chest in relief and gratitude that the cause of alarm wasn't something much worse.

If the cook dropped a pan on the floor and exclaimed, "Puppalapup!" or some such nonsense, my aunts would jump and repeat, "Puppalapup!" or whatever else he may have said.

This skittishness took preposterous forms, and Shan did his best to provoke them. He would come up stealthily behind Lily, and at the moment of startling her would say something like: "Dear me, I simply have to stand here and take a pee." And, jumping, she would repeat, "Dear me, I simply have to stand here and take a pee." Shan was waiting for the day when he could get our aunts to do, not just say, whatever was suggested to them in their brief hypnotic state. But Lily always caught herself in time and, coming to her senses, would giggle and slap him on the shoulder.

Or he would pounce on Rosie and do a clown's dance,

whereupon she would follow, abandoning all dignity until she had recovered her wits.

This peculiar reflex mimicry was not uncommon; the cook, for example, could be jolted time and again into his own bizarre version. As often as you set the trap, he fell into it. You had only to say, "Minnow, tell me your recipe for potato cutlet." Then, when he began, "You take three potatoes and smash them . . . " all you had to do was poke him in the ribs and he would jump and spit out the naughty words over which he swore he had no control: " . . . and then you take some pussy hairs and pound them in with the potatoes . . . "

My aunts had never been victims of this malady, and I wondered now if they weren't playing a kind of necessary game by feigning these "seizures."

About this time, other falsehoods, equally puzzling, were coming to light. In telling his stories, Shan seemed no longer to make distinctions between the actual and the imagined. He would sit at the table and feed us his flummery and yarns. He spun fables of discovery, achievement, power, and wealth—how he planned to dive for sunken treasures of gold, rubies, and sapphires; how he would scale the snow mountains for the rare and priceless coffin tree—as though ticking off items on a routine agenda. And oddly enough my aunts, who knew as well as I that he was making things up, would keep a straight face and nod permissively. I never understood their indulgence; and whenever I challenged him, they would silence me with a little gesture of the hand or the head as if to say, "Let him! What harm is there?"

There was no harm; it was only entertainment. But there was a theme—and a resolution—to most of his stories. The theme was violence and the resolution was in his emergence as hero. These stories were usually about street gangs representing good and evil: His friends (the good gang) had been walking amiably along the river one day, when half a dozen thugs had picked a fight with them; and Shan, seeking justice, had returned to the same spot the next day and taken on the aggressors single-handedly, until they were all doubled up in pain or bleeding and begging for mercy.

Or, by popular request from his dockyard friends, he had gone up to the slave driver of a foreman, given him the rough side of his tongue and his fist, which landed the quaking foreman in a barrel of tar.

As he talked, I looked for evidence of these scuffles and brawls he claimed to have survived; but there were no bruises on his high forehead, no scars on his smooth cheeks, no cuts on his soft, expressive hands.

Alone with me, he was less of a braggart. He played the guitar, or sang, or clasped his hands behind his head, daydreaming, or said, teasing: "Come and tell me your hopes and fears; they put me to sleep."

His inventions were only a part of the pretenses that all of us in the family had agreed in some unspoken way to live by. Though I was nearly twenty, my aunts still pretended I was a child. Uncle, a married man with six children, pretended to be a bachelor. Shan pretended he was a fearless champion of the weak and the preyed upon. And everyone pretended that Father's absence was only temporary.

Even as I wondered if I would ever see my father again, I too kept up the pretense and never asked. I had learned in any case that it was unproductive to nurse any curiosity about my parents; they were off limits to me.

But how can I trust myself now to get to the roots of ills suffered in so distant a past? Perhaps I place the blame for all those boarded-up misgivings on a family trait when it was as much my own fear of knowing the difficult truth that made me an accomplice to deceit.

And so it was years before I could even admit to myself the suspicions that my father aroused in me but that I never allowed to surface.

I think, for example, of that day of the coup when those anonymous uniformed men came looking for him. Relieved though I was that the search had been harmless, it left me guessing and uneasy. It was as if they were already well aware that Father had gone into hiding, yet felt it necessary to stage that theater with the trucks and the armed troops. They were after Father in earnest—the subsequent arrests of the cabinet were proof—but they must have known that the means to capturing him lay nowhere in his house; not even in seizing his children, whom they allowed instead to go on sleeping.

The enemy must have sensed that Father would not have let flesh and blood thwart his determination. When they left us alone, they must have realized—as I have come to acknowledge only now, after all these years—that they could have gone to any lengths to hold us hostage; but if he felt forced into a contest of wills, he would never have given in. Faced with that challenge, he would have gritted his teeth—or rather bit his tongue the way he did in the throes of fury—and simply sat out the ordeal.

Father wasn't so easily swayed from a course of action, political or moral, he had set for himself. He had wars to win and wrongs to right, children or no. He had that kind of calling.

At the time, of course, I was largely in the dark about the nature of his calling. I could rattle off by rote the catchwords describing his ideals: Independence for the Hill States, Freedom from Oppression, Liberation from the Tyranny of the Central Government. He had spent close to thirty years of his life in the service of those goals. He had founded the legendary guerrilla force, the People's Army. But beyond this official version of what he stood for, I knew almost nothing about his life. I was aware of the secrecy and danger that set his mission apart from the jobs other fathers did for a living; but I understood little and questioned even less.

Still, for all my careful indifference, now and then some chance discovery would bring home to me the utter affront of Father's dedication to a cause so removed from his family. I am thinking of the day the maid came home with some lentil fritters she had bought at a sidewalk stall. She offered me the last few pieces, and when I came to the bottom of the paper cone, I unfurled it. Sometimes these scraps of paper used by the vendors to wrap food in were pages torn out of discarded exercise books that had belonged to school-children, and I liked to study the smeared fragments of theorems or compositions on the oil-stained page—and feel a pang of something like homesickness for school. (I missed being able to lose myself in subjects that stood apart from reality.)

The paper this time was of a different stock—porous and coarse, like the cover of a pulp novel. The print was small and the block of text ran askew. I describe it so exactly because I have it in hand now, ten years later. It was a propaganda sheet, but as the only justification of my father's cause I had seen in print, it seemed a document worth saving.

PEOPLE'S ARMY ELIMINATES HEAD-HUNTING
IN NORTHERN STATES

From the testimony of a village elder:

"Some months ago, I had a bad shock. It was at an exhibition in the northeast. The central government was celebrating its second anniversary, and the exhibition was part of the ceremonies. I was part of the northern district delegation.

On the table, in the middle of a booth, were human skulls and two rusty swords used in head-hunting. This reminded me of my childhood experience of attending a head-hunting ceremony. It was held in the shade of a huge tree. There were some wooden drums and a forked pillar on which buffalo heads were hanging. There were also pillars with human skulls on top.

I looked at the human skulls, wondering if my mother's was among them, for she was beheaded while harvesting paddy about 20 years earlier.

I did not know at that time who started this custom and why. I thought it was tradition.

In those days, we believed all sorts of things. The sorcerers and landlords told us that we had to bribe the spirits for rain and good harvest. We had to bribe them with slaughtered buffalo. The same landlords made us believe that paddy which is not watered by blood is inferior in quality.

But the poor people in the villages could not afford to slaughter buffalo or cows for sacrifices to the spirits! Only landlords could afford it. And these landlords told the villagers that if they could not slaughter buffalo to appease the spirits for the sake of the entire village, they must hunt human heads. They offered to hold buffalo slaughtering ceremonies if the villagers could get human heads. This is how the custom started.

So the head-hunters, after beheading people, would put the heads into shoulder bags and rush back (because of great humidity and high heat) to the place where the ceremony would be held.

This custom brought about battles between villages and made the villagers depend more on the landlords for protection. Thus, the landlords became more powerful.

Now I know that head-hunting is an instrument for class oppression. The custom was started by the reactionary lowland government to protect their ruling class and their exploitation of the Hill States. The illegal military clique now in power is no different.

But things have changed in the Hill States. Since the

birth of the People's Army 20 years ago, and as a result of the People's Democratic Revolution, gone is the head-hunting custom of the northern states.

Although I cannot replace my mother's head, I am satisfied that the custom has been eliminated from our region."

So this was what Father had abandoned us for: a fight to stamp out some barbaric practice in the alien outposts of our country. It disturbed me beyond reason to dwell on that thought. All of a sudden it seemed to me not just regrettable but downright wrong for him to be mixed up in the fate of strangers that should not have concerned him. Let them hunt heads! What business of his was it? His business was to be a father to us, his children; why else had he given us life? An unfamiliar rush of anger brought an ache to my throat and a sting to my eyes. Was I brought into this world to vie with headhunters for my father's attention?

But suppose, by miracle, he were to return home to stay. What could I have offered him? I pictured him restless, pacing the floor, or pressed against a window, staring past me, past the trees, the lawn, the lake, into a distance that was free from home and its encumbrances. And what could I have given him then, to make up for all his losses?

It was better not to ask these questions. It was better to remain fogbound, to try not to notice what could not be changed—just as people could walk through the streets of our city and seem not to notice the signs of creeping decay: treetops growing out of houses; elephant grass sprouting out of building walls; parks and gardens overgrown with weed; beggars and sick children scavenging in the trash heaps.

These were the conditions that prevailed three years after Father had gone underground, and all the news we could hope for was the sporadic messages from him assuring us that he was well and praying we were the same, or directing us on some pressing household matter. These were the conditions we had come to accept when one of Father's men arrived early one morning to put us on a plane bound for the border.

Arrangements for our journey had been made; palms had been greased. We had only to pack a small bag with essentials for the trip. Everything else could be purchased later.

So complete was our obedience that we sprang out of bed and did as we were told, never even stopping to ask the obvious questions until we were at the front door and Uncle volunteered the information, almost as an afterthought, that Father had arranged this flight because war and bloodshed were in the wind, and he wanted us safely in America.

"It's only for a while, just for a while," he kept saying. "You'll be free in America. You'll be out of danger. And we're too old to bother them. We'll be safe here. We'll look after things."

When we had climbed into the waiting jeep, our aunts clung to our wrists, unable to speak. Rosie's face looked shrunken and shocked. Uncle was stammering: something about how we would at least get an education. Lily finally was able to say, "Go, then; go if you must!" as if any of it were our doing.

This was our farewell to home.

4

____

Even when times were hard, the life we left behind had run along a groove cut by tradition, familiarity, and habit. But arriving in New York, my brother and I fell out of that groove, and finding our footing was nearly as awkward as the astronauts' first steps in the atmosphere of the moon.

We landed in America three months after they landed on the moon and watched the event on a giant television screen that hung above the maze of cosmetics and costume jewelry in a Fifth Avenue store. It was our first American department store, but the visit was short-lived. After several runs of the moon footage we had wandered into the women's shoe department, where we tried to beat down the price of a pair of sandals, bazaar-style.

"How much are these?"

"Twenty-five dollars."

"I'll give you seventeen."

"Excuse me?"

"All right, twenty."

The saleswoman began to treat us like morons, shouting, "Twenty-five! Twenty-five! Twenty-five!" Red-faced, we abandoned the sandals and the store.

We had arrived with two bags of lightweight clothing and five hundred dollars in cash. In his message instructing us to leave the country, Father had said we should get in touch with Morrison, a friend who lived in New York, and explain our circumstances. He would give us what help we needed. In the meantime, he would be sending us more money in Morrison's care to tide us over our first few months.

But contacting this man was harder than we had imagined. The letter we wrote him came back ten days later marked: MOVED. ADDRESS UNKNOWN. We didn't have a telephone number, and when we looked through the directory there were enough Morrisons to make us despair.

We must have called fifty different numbers before reaching the one that seemed likeliest. But we couldn't be certain, because it was a recording.

The voice bore a promising resemblance to what we remembered of Morrison's. But how to make sense out of the recording? Was it a joke or a trick or a code? So we took turns redialing and hanging up with each beep.

In those early days it seemed as if we had been thrown into a colossal obstacle course where machinery, gadgetry, and mystery of one sort or another stood in our way at every turn. All around us, hordes of people were breezing through those same obstacles without a second thought: waiting for the right buses, running down the right entrances to the subways, dropping the right change into the right slots, not even needing to look up from their papers to get off at the right stops, pushing the right buttons on elevators, giving their orders at restaurants and cafeterias in the right voices, the right words. We had had glimpses of these marvels in the movies back home, but seeing an elevator on film is inadequate preparation for stepping into one for the first time without getting crushed by the heavy, ineluctable doors, and then recovering in time to press the right button.

We kept calling the number with the recording for weeks, though prevented by an inexpressible shyness from saying a word. And when at last a real voice answered, we hung up again—from habit. But when we plucked up the nerve to call back, the miraculous happened: We had found our Morrison.

It wasn't quite the exchange we'd expected. Instead of offering to pick us up immediately and take us back to his home, he invited us to dinner—and on a day that was three weeks away. From that brief exchange, we should have guessed that Morrison knew nothing of Father's promised funds. But we couldn't be sure. Maybe he thought it improper to raise the subject over the telephone. (We came from a purse-proud society where talk of money had its own rules of decorum.) Maybe he was waiting till we met in person. We would just have to wait.

But the dinner invitation brought its own set of worries. What would we wear? What would we talk about? What subjects should we try to evade, for fear of revealing our ignorance about things that concerned our still unsorted past, our shaky present, our even shakier future?

By lucky accident we had managed to find a run-down but reasonably priced hotel on the Upper West Side. The desk clerk there, who had advised us on other matters, told us that the best bargains for clothing could be found along Orchard and Mulberry streets, so we walked up and down those blocks, combing through the racks for clothes both affordable and appropriate. Years later, I came across a cartoon that reminded me of our bumbling stabs at presentability. It showed a cloddish-looking fellow in a folksy costume and a belled cap, holding a tambourine and saying, "And now I will sing you a song of my country."

So must we have seemed when we arrived at the Morrisons' Park Avenue address: Shan in his shiny suit that drooped at the shoulders, I in my lime green dress with shoes to match—a pair of bumpkins singing a song of our country.

When I was growing up, Morrison had been an occasional visitor, always arriving crumpled and sweaty from the long ride in from the airport, but full of laughter and loaded with presents. Now, on his turf, he greeted us at the door with brisk handshakes—not the exuberant embraces we were used to. Admittedly, five years had passed since we had seen him last. He had been a bachelor then, a ruddy-faced man in safari shirts with a startlingly loud laugh. Now, in his dark suit, he was older and paler and far from uproarious.

I heard other voices in the room beyond and discovered with a sinking heart that we were not the only guests. Mrs. Morrison came forward to greet us. She held out the tips of her fingers as if expecting them to be kissed. She was very thin, with broad, freckled shoulders that jutted out above a strapless black dress. Her eyes were sunken and seemed to require an effort to stay open; her cheeks were hollow; her smile hinted at disappointment. She led us across several Persian carpets into the living room. The introductions made, she promptly turned her back on us and resumed the conversation we had apparently interrupted, which had to do with the difficulty of flying in fresh salmon from Alaska.

Morrison seemed at a loss for words. We were faces out of a past he didn't appear eager to recall. Perhaps he no longer wished to dabble in the politics of our country. Perhaps he had seen the writing on the wall when, after the long summer he spent in Father's rebel camp, he returned to the United States to raise funds for the cause, only to raise a shipment of used grade-school texts for the children of the rebel villages.

Whatever the reasons, he seemed almost as ill-at-ease at

his own dinner table as we were, sitting there in our chintzy clothes, while the Japanese butler smirked at our hesitations over the linen and silver. Unequal to the level and pace of conversation, we remained mute, regretting the mistake of our presence there.

We made our escape as soon as we could, refusing a cab with the excuse that we preferred to walk. The coats we still couldn't afford we claimed to have left at home. ("No, no, we like the cold!"—we who had grown up in tropical heat.)

Outside, we shivered in the autumn wind and walked with bowed heads all the thirty blocks home.

The next day we steeled ourselves to make the odious telephone call asking about the money Father was supposed to have sent. It fell to me, the younger, the brasher of the two, to call. The indecency of asking for money (though rightfully ours) would be mitigated, we agreed, coming from me.

It was such a simple question: Had the Morrisons by chance received some money from Father? And yet it took some twelve hours of hesitation and argument to make that call. It took repeated rehearsals of that single line for me to collect the nerve.

Over the telephone, and without the appeasement of her tired smile, Mrs. Morrison's voice had the unfaltering resonance of a radio announcer. It was the Voice of America. I managed to deliver my well-rehearsed query. On the other end, there was a pause; and then a deep breath.

"You know, my dear," she said, her voice taking on the coziness of a nanny reading a bedtime story, "Mr. Morrison and I have not been involved with your part of the world for many years now. We've had no contact, financial or otherwise. We certainly know nothing about these funds from your father. Surely you don't think we'd be sitting on it if we had it? Now, we know it isn't easy for you and your brother here, so far away from home. You come from a proud family; it must be hard for you to ask for help. But I personally believe it is always better to speak openly and directly. Why not come right out and say you need money? Then maybe we could work something out."

I could think of no other response than to drop the phone. "I told you we shouldn't have asked," I said to Shan, blaming him for the humiliation.

When I told him what had happened, he bit his lip in anger. It was at moments like these that Father's spirit seemed to possess his face. Otherwise, they were not really alike at all.

Father was not a tall man, but he had no need for height. He carried himself with the assurance of a natural bully. All his expressions—the way he lifted his chin, the way he moved his mouth—spelt braggadocio. From a distance, his small hooded eyes seemed set in a humorous slant, but up close they flashed every kind of threat. His head was too big for his body, but even this disproportion was right. It had the logic of a mythic creature: the head of a lion on the body of a buck.

Shan was half a head taller than Father, but it was a smaller, more delicate head. He had Father's thick lips, which could curl up with similar bravado, but on the whole his features were set on a feminine scale, which robbed him of the forceful look.

My aunts used to say about Shan, "Look at those lovely long lashes. All that thick curly hair. He should have been a girl."

"Bloody stupid woman," Shan said now, still smarting from Mrs. Morrison's insult. "Just like that woman at the train station."

I had heard the story before: how when he was a boy— this was after he had come south—he had seen, at a train station, a beggar woman dragging herself about on her hands. She was not only crippled but crazed, and had attracted, like some zoo animal, a small audience that threw things at her: coins, nuts, bottle caps, sticks, and stones. The trick she performed was to dart at the flying debris, catch it in mid-air, and, after a quick appraisal, tuck it into her ragged bodice. When the object turned out to be a bottle cap rather than a coin, she spat and hissed, her shoulders swaying with the taut movements of a cobra poised to strike.

Suddenly, distracted by a new face, the beggar turned her back on the crowd. At the edge of the platform close to the trains, a white woman as tall as a man was sitting on a pile of suitcases.

The beggar moved toward her, scraping the ground as she went with a broken razor blade. The woman with the suitcases began to notice the approaching cripple with her mysterious scrapings and looked this way and that, uneasily.

The beggar kept scratching away, until she reached the woman's feet. There she deposited the little mound of dirt she had scraped along, with a flourish that betokened an extravagant gift. Flustered, the white woman reached into her purse, threw a folded money bill at the beggar, and hurriedly dragged her bags toward the train.

The beggar had made no move to pick up the money; but as the tall woman threw her suitcases up onto one of the cars and climbed in, she bounded after her, racing on her hands, and, shouting out a string of vile abuse, flung the note at the woman's back.

"Stupid foreigners," Shan said. "They think money is everything."

"We're the foreigners now," I reminded him. "We're the men on the moon."

We moved to a cheaper place—a certain Hotel Macy on Broadway near Times Square. In the narrow lobby we rubbed shoulders with its floating clientele of junkies, pimps, and whores. The air was so thick with marijuana that the sweet fumes clung to our clothes.

But our room was a double with a four-burner gas range, utensils included. We cooked whatever went on sale at the corner grocery store: dented cans of string beans or mushroom soup; a head of discolored cabbage; a packet of lentils. But the mainstay was rice: We had a pot of it daily as a base for the meager toppings. Occasionally, when hot dogs went on sale, there would be meat on the table: one sausage per meal, diced small, heavily camouflaged with curry powder and garlic, and mixed in with the rice.

Money was dwindling, but sometimes, walking past a cafeteria, we stopped to study the menus pasted to the window and broke down under the assault of the greasy, oniony odors. Inside, we attacked our $1.25 specials of meat loaf with savage concentration, resuming talk only when the last smudge of gravy had disappeared—and then regretting our haste.

The wonder of our first snow! We stood at the corner of Lexington and Twenty-third and held out our palms to the falling snowflakes—the way we beckoned to the pigeons back home.

Then came the rush of the crippling cold: the piercing air, the wind lashing through our cheap, foam-lined loden coats, our aching toes inside the rubber boots, the fear for our fingers and ears. We wanted never to leave our garlicky, overheated room.

Working in tandem out of fear and insecurity, we went as a pair in search of work, one of us waiting outside while the other was interviewed. We were so poorly prepared for the tests of survival in a changed habitat that we started out with blind ambition—blind to our own limitations.

At first we circled the want ads in the *Times*'s clerical and sales columns, but after the repeated rejections, we lowered our sights until we sank to the grind of washing dishes and waiting on tables at any restaurant that would hire us as a pair.

Christmas came with its frantic commercial festivity. Dazzled by the window displays of opulence such as occurred only in dreams, we could walk along, on our days off, for hours at a time and almost forget the cold.

On Christmas Eve, we stayed in our room and listened to the drama of two streetwalkers quarreling outside and two men ending an affair in the room next door.

In the drawer of the rusty cabinet under the kitchen sink, Shan found a roll of green insulating tape ("insulting tape," he read in his careless way), which he cut into strips and stuck to the window in a Christmas tree design of inverted V's.

The next morning, three lumpy packages wrapped in aluminum foil awaited me on the windowsill: a hairbrush, a pair of woolen tights, and a knitted cap.

A rough calculation of how much those three items had cost made me tremble: There was a week's worth of groceries. I said, "We can't eat these. Why did you do it?"

I may as well have wiped my feet on his presents.

"So we'll starve," he said and began to peel off the green tape from the window. "But at least one of us won't freeze."

I went into the bathroom, where I stood over the sink for a long time, washing my face again and again until I had composed myself.

"What's the matter?" he asked, noticing my red eyes.

"Nothing. I got soap in my eyes."

We pretended all was well. I brushed my hair with the new brush, put on the tights and the cap, and suggested a walk through the snow.

Lying across a sidewalk was a scraggly pine tree still draped with tinsel and stiff with sprayed-on snow. Underneath its branches, we found a portable typewriter in a boxy case and carried it home. The *q* was missing and the spacing erratic, but the carriage was sound.

I bought a typing manual and tapped out the lessons in

the evenings. Shan memorized the keyboard. With two fingers, he could make better time than I, but he soon tired of the exercise and went to bed early, while I continued to pick out my lessons at night.

Braver now, I left him in our room one afternoon and went to a succession of interviews that would take several hours. By then it would be dark, so we arranged to meet at six in the evening, at a halfway point, and from there to walk home together.

Snow was coming down in a drizzle scarcely distinguishable from rain when I stood at the corner where we were to meet. Although Christmas was past, a Salvation Army Santa Claus stamped his fireman's boots in the gray slush and shook a bell, first in one hand, then in the other. The store window behind me was festooned with plastic sandals that seemed crafted out of colored glass. Six o'clock had passed without any sign of Shan. Another half hour went by. I walked up and down the block, stopping under the lamp lights to look up at the insects of snow swarming around the light.

I wanted to find a telephone booth but was afraid of missing him. At seven o'clock, finally, I took the risk and went to call the "hotel." The front desk rang our room. No answer. I ran back to my spot, fearing he had come and gone, waited another ten minutes, then ran back to the phone booth again. Still no answer. Distraught, I rushed back to the corner and, looking down the street, saw him at last. He was hurrying through the crowds, a halo of ice around his forehead.

"What happened? I've been going crazy!" My teeth were chattering from cold and relief.

"I fell asleep. I don't know what's wrong with me."

We started down the street back toward the hotel. "Asleep! How could you sleep for so long, leaving me out in the cold like that? I almost called the police."

"Police!" He looked at me fearfully. "Don't ever start anything with the police in this country. They do what they want. Say you're driving along in a car and they stop you? If you don't freeze at once, they blow your head off."

I stopped him. He was out of breath and incoherent. "What's the matter? You look sick."

"I don't know," he said, puzzled himself. "I slept as if I died."

That day marked a new pattern for him: of chronic tiredness and drowsiness.

Weeks later, one of my countless interviews bore fruit. The new job paid a pittance, but it required nothing more than sorting mail and operating a Xerox machine. And from the coffee room I could smuggle out packets of hot chocolate, dried milk, coffee, tea, sugar, and Saltine crackers.

At home, it was I who consumed most of it. Shan's appetite had fallen off. Complaining of aches and chills that came and went erratically, he scarcely left his bed. One night I was awakened by a pounding beside me: his whole bed was electrified and throbbing from the violence of his chill. I covered him with a heap of bedsheets and blankets and both our coats, but he continued to shiver and babble.

The next morning his temperature had dropped, but he could barely stand up by himself.

He had been so drenched in sweat during the night that I had spread newspapers over the damp sheets. But the papers, too, were soon soaked through and in the end I had stripped the sheets and soaked them in the bathtub. They were lying now in water that was gray with newsprint.

There was no place to hang the sheets out to dry, so after wringing them out, I carried them to work in plastic bags.

On the way, I decided it was time to tap our last emergency reserve. I unscrewed the pearls from my ears and stopped off at a pawnshop, where in return for the earrings

I walked away with a ticket and twenty-five dollars in cash.

It was the briefest of transactions—and it covered the cost of a physician's house call.

I was already late for work, and by the time I had made the calls to locate a doctor, the morning was almost gone while the office mail was still unsorted. I rushed through the pile as best I could and left at lunchtime with my plastic bags of wet sheets, heading for the nearest laundromat.

While the sheets were in the washer, I called home and learned that the doctor had come and gone. The provisional diagnosis was, as we had suspected, malaria.

I left the clothes in the washer, took the subway home to pick up the prescription the doctor had written, rushed back to the laundromat to throw the sheets into the dryer, and went to fill the prescription at a drugstore. When I returned to the laundromat, the sheets had been taken out of the dryer and were lying on the table, still damp. The plastic bags were gone, so I folded the sheets hurriedly and raced back to the office.

As luck determined, I walked into the same elevator as the office manager, who took in the sheets with an inquiring glance but said nothing. When I reached my desk in the mailroom, I found a note asking to see me in his office.

All that rushing around had made me absentminded: I carried the pile of bedsheets in with me.

"Let me get to the point," he said. "Are you holding another job?"

I opened my mouth to speak and found myself dissolving from a stammer into a chuckle.

"You may think because we are a friendly group here that we have time for games," he went on. "If so, you have the wrong impression. I've been watching you and I've noticed, a number of us have noticed, that you've been coming in late, taking long lunches, and generally, well, falling down on the job.

"I can't tell you how disappointed I am. You came in here with no credentials to speak of, and I hired you on faith. Faith, yes, and because I sensed there was more to you than meets the eye. I had a feeling about you. I hoped you'd be a kind of iron butterfly. Now I hate to say this, but you've turned out to be just a butterfly, flitting in and out. I can't understand it. You're a bright girl, basically, and I know that most Oriental people are honest and hardworking. I've seen many others who've come here from your part of the world —real go-getters, starting from scratch and making it. But you've got to want to be somebody. You've got to have values. I can't teach you commitment. You've got to be committed yourself."

His voice dropped. "I'm sorry. You don't cut the mustard. I'm afraid we're going to have to let you go."

I stood up and gathered the damp sheets. "If I don't cut the mustard, why are you afraid?" I said, light-headed with defiance.

The office manager reddened. "It's an expression," he said. "Someday, when your English is better, you'll understand it."

I called Shan to tell him I'd be home early. He assumed I was simply taking the afternoon off.

"I'll make dinner," he said. "I feel much better. Just tell me what to cook."

I hadn't eaten all day and was limp with hunger, but hesitant about letting him cook. "Are you sure?"

"Shooooer," he said playfully, to let me know he was in good spirits.

I could smell the garlic the minute I walked through the door of the lobby at the Hotel Macy. The cloud thickened with each flight of stairs I climbed. Shan answered my knock with a ladle in his hand. "It's all done," he said. "You can eat. But I think I put a little too much garlic in it."

I opened the pot of curried mushroom soup and reeled.

Beside the stove, the bottle of garlic powder lay open, its perforated top by its side. I saw that the powder level had gone down almost an inch since I'd last used it.

"I was shaking the garlic powder and the top fell into the soup," he explained.

"Never mind," I said. "Let's eat."

"You eat," he said. "I already ate."

"I've already eaten," I corrected him churlishly as I piled my dish with rice and topped it with the gummy soup.

I took my first mouthful and gagged. The garlic had the potency of ammonia. I set the plate down. "I can't eat this. A dog can't eat this."

"There's nothing else," he said in a small voice. "I'll make you hot chocolate?"

"I'm sick of hot chocolate," I said. "I'm sick of crackers. I just wanted rice and soup. I've been starving."

"I'm sorry," he said. "Really sorry. I know how hungry you are."

"I lost the job," I told him.

"What? Why?"

"I didn't cut the mustard."

"What mustard?"

"You see? Our English just isn't good enough."

I picked up the plate again and took a deep breath. Barely chewing the mouthfuls of rice, I swallowed the food until I gagged again.

"This is so horrible," I burst out, spraying a mouthful of rice onto the floor.

He took my plate away and knelt beside me. "I'm feeling better now," he said. "Soon I'll get a job and we'll be all right. Wait and see."

And he started to pick up the grains of rice from the floor, saying, "This place has enough rats already."

5

Father had given us the name of one other contact, an American journalist who over the years had spent time in his camps and returned to file reports sympathetic to the rebel cause. But the Morrison episode had left us chary of seeking him out. After six months of flophouse existence, however —six months of hot chocolate, canned soups, and menial jobs, with Shan's bout of cerebral malaria as the culmination —we were ready to take our chances again.

Benjamin Lane, the journalist, lived in a large brownstone in the East Seventies. Quick to assess our penury, he and his wife, Matty, took us into their chaotic household of eight children, rotating in-laws, dogs, cats, and macaws. We had a room to ourselves in the basement, divided by a warped coromandel screen and warmed by frayed rugs and quilts and furniture from the attic. After the Hotel Macy it had the feel of a hot drink on a cold night.

Shamed by our circumstances, we kept our privations to

ourselves, but it was clear that we were down and out ("down and out without a paddle" as Shan used to say). We made ourselves useful in minor ways. Shan found an old guitar, sang to the children, and taught them to play. I read to them, or walked the dogs. Too poor to afford a movie or a meal out, we remained homebound, serving in effect as full-time caretakers.

Yet I felt the strain created by our presence. The longer we stayed, the keener was my sense of being there on sufferance, of needing to shrink into an unobtrusive object.

I could have taken greater pains to join in the domestic bustle, but the truth was that I had grown up with no serviceable skills to speak of—domestic or otherwise. Everyone had assumed that my future lay some place other than in the home, though where that might be no one thought to anticipate. Rather than reveal my helplessness to the Lanes, I tried to stay out of the way.

The size and sheer rambunctiousness of their family gave me palpitations in any case. I wasn't used to the routine brawls (between children and parents, children and children, or parent and parent); to the back talk, the shouting matches, the swings of emotion between Matty and Ben (his sarcastic tauntings, her tears of frustration, their sudden reconciliations followed by hugs and kisses); to the offhand brutality of a large family.

Shan and I retreated to the basement at every opportunity, where we could whisper about this or that slight we had imagined. In reality the Lanes' only offense against us was that they might not have known the extent of our defeat. At worst they might have mistaken our stealth for something other than simple inadequacy.

In our spreading suspicions, even the children began to pose threats. Their blond smells, their unregulated tantrums, their abuse of our politeness (especially in the presence of their parents, where they sensed our deference), made us as wary of them as of a band of playful but vicious monkeys.

The only exception was Danny, the adopted child, a five-year-old Cherokee whose blunt haircut and broad face held out to us some hint of kinship, and whose slanted eyes watched us with an indefinable flicker of recognition. He would stand outside our door and announce himself in his husky voice: "This Danny," or lie flat on the floor, spread-eagle and eye-level with the crack under our door, his ear pressed to the ground, inquiring, "What doin'?"

Months passed. Aimless, rootless, full of inadmissible fears, we withdrew into our self-made limbo, convinced that the Lanes were counting the hours until our departure. We imagined them gossiping among their friends and complaining about the burden we posed. We thought they refrained from speaking their minds only out of the same sense of decorum and politeness by which we ourselves were so strictly and senselessly governed.

In the beginning, before we were on the lookout for slights and innuendo, it was understood that we would join the family every evening for dinner. In time, somehow even this routine became a matter of daily speculation on our part: Were we expected at the table? Had they tired of the two extra mouths to feed? Were we disrupting the intimacy of the family? Should we pretend we'd already eaten? If we left the house at the right moment and wandered about the neighborhood, we could claim to have eaten when Matty or one of the children knocked on our door to announce dinner. Then, later, much later at night when the parents had left for an after-dinner drink with friends and the children were safely in bed, we could steal upstairs and raid the kitchen for a spoonful, a handful of leftovers that wouldn't be missed.

One evening, when we had the house to ourselves, we gathered a bundle of raw pasta taken from half a dozen opened packages, cooked it hurriedly, and tossed it in an old pan with olive oil and butter in amounts that would escape inventory. Seizing the moment, we added a cupful of cooked rice and sprinkled over this unappetizing mishmash a package of raisins which someone had thrown, unopened, into the garbage. Our hope was that we could get through the next several days without accepting an invitation to dinner.

The concoction fed us for three nights running. We ate off the pan, which stayed hidden under my bed. (By now, I was used to carrying most of the risks. The role had been assigned through an unspoken agreement that, if caught, I would be better at bluffing.)

To this day, my palate recalls the oily aftertaste of that cold pasta, raisins, and rice—awful enough now, as then, to bring tears to the eyes. But that stolen meal bought us a few days of bogus pride; it allowed us the illusion of fending for ourselves.

When next we permitted ourselves to join the Lanes for dinner, it was with a group of their friends they had invited back from an office cocktail party. After dinner, when most of the dishes had been cleared away, I leaned over and saw Shan locked in conversation with a photographer. I couldn't hear what they were saying, but something in their respective expressions—Shan's nervousness, the photographer's bemusement—made me strain to decipher the conversation. I must have transmitted a signal without knowing it, for in the next instant everyone else had stopped talking to listen to the exchange at the end of the table.

Shan was saying, "Look, man, the CIA was in my country so I know." His slangy tone made me sit up; it was so unlike the measured inflections he took care to use among strangers.

"They've taken over everything. Opium and everything. They know who's going to be boss one day and who's going to bugger off the next day. So you tell me there's no CIA in your office?"

The photographer was taking his time stubbing out a cigarette in the ashtray. "I'm not sure what your point is," he said without looking up.

Glances were exchanged. Ben gave a clownish shrug and laughed. A woman with a coat she had kept on through dinner—a coat that could have passed for a hair shirt—rolled her eyes and reached for a bottle of wine. Matty got up from the table and stopped at Shan's chair on her way to the kitchen.

"You're wonderful," she said, laughing and ruffling his hair. "If only I could understand you."

Shan swung around with a look of wild exasperation and leaned back too far in his seat. He went down on his back with a crash.

I jumped up to help. "See what happens when you drink too much?" I said. The laughter was loud enough so that I wasn't sure I could be heard. "See what happens when you drink too much?" I kept repeating.

Smiling inanely in my humiliation, I led him downstairs. My heart was racing with confusion. I knew he hadn't drunk enough to justify that outburst.

"What in God's name is wrong with you?" I said, the minute the door was closed. "Making us look like idiots!"

He looked at me with hatred so new and direct that I recoiled. "Shan! God, what's wrong?"

"What the hell do you know about anything?" he said, his head cocked in contempt. "These people are all CIA."

"Are you crazy? Where do you get these ideas? Why didn't you say anything to me before? Why make a fool of yourself?"

"Fool? The fool is you. The fool is them. You don't know. And they think I don't know. Ah, forget it," he trailed off, waving away something invisible in the air. "I'm going to sleep."

The next day, he claimed to have no recollection of the incident.

But I noticed that he was spending more time in bed—not always asleep, but dozing lightly, or at any rate determined to lie there with eyes shut, arms folded, meditative. His talk now revolved around some outlandish money-making scheme. In these moments of woolgathering, I detected the same look he used to have at the poker tables back home: eyes narrowed in acute expectation that at any moment a mere downward flick of a winning hand would bring him the luck that had played fast and loose with him for most of his life.

Luck meant the success of a windfall momentous enough to warrant the long wait, the gamble, the immobilizing fantasies. The schemes that were undertaken in pursuit of that windfall! I remembered the hot days of the monsoon season turning into clammy sunsets as I sat on the raft, anxious, wet, and shivering, waiting for the metal dome of his homemade compressed-air tank to break the still surface of the lake.

These were dry runs for what were to be soundings in the open sea for sunken treasures which he believed were there for the harvesting. ("I've talked to fishermen, boatmen; don't ask me these stupid questions.")

The diving apparatus had flaws that were never fixed. The open sea was never reached. But the lure of treasures, the pipe dreams, persisted. One day his luck would change, bringing power, riches, and the means to use or abuse them on a kingly scale.

Meanwhile, in the cocoon of the Lanes' basement, he found excuses to push aside the urgency of finding a job. I had given up combing the want ads for him and focused now on the ones with potential for myself alone.

With audacity born of desperation, I reported to an employment agency. The woman in charge took in my appearance with the assessing look of a judge at a beauty contest and shook her head. "Those shoes. Where did you get them?"

They were the same pair of sandals I had left home in.

"Where?" She repeated the name of my country once, twice, three times, casting about in her mind for some connection with a face, a place, but drawing a blank and dismissing the mystery with a shrug.

She questioned me on the jobs I had held, the ones I had applied for but failed to secure. After a while, she set her pencil down and her face softened. She smiled. "I have just the job for you. Clerical. A big chemical company. I have this feeling about you. You could be a smartie. But you've got a ways to go, darling. Those shoes! You shouldn't be seen dead in them, much less go to an interview wearing them. They'd fire you before they hired you. You want me to be straight, right?"

She took off her own shoes, black pumps of fake alligator, and pushed them toward me. "Here, take those off and wear mine. We don't have time."

I could barely get my feet into them.

"Look, we're not talking comfort. We're talking necessity, darling. This is a big job. So you suffer a little inconvenience. Just go in there and get that job."

I arrived at the interview with pains shooting through my feet and limped behind the receptionist as she led me into the office of the personnel manager. He was a dark, reedy-looking man with an Italian name and the kind of mustache worn by villains in the open-air theaters staged back home. He seemed surprisingly relaxed, a man with time on his hands. After the pleasantries, he settled back in his chair. "Tell me," he said, "what you think are your strongest and your weakest points."

I had been through so many unsuccessful screenings in which I had edited my opinions, to no avail, that I decided to try a different tack. I would make up in bold honesty what I lacked in credentials. Here was a man obviously used to getting the stock answers, the expedient lies fostered by such a line of questioning. I would show a little spunk.

"To start with the weak points," I said, "I don't much care for work. I was never trained for any kind of job, but I think that's only part of it. Maybe I'm just lazy. I lack direction. Also I am forgetful. I make mistakes. On the other hand," I went on, encouraged by the slow, satanic, incredulous chuckle that was escaping him, "I am in terrible need. I have no money, and I think this will make me willing to learn and to work."

Still laughing, he tipped his chair backwards and glanced under the desk. I had taken the plastic-alligator shoes off and was flexing my toes. This seemed to heighten his humor.

He stood up. "Let me take you on a tour through our offices."

"Oh, no!" I said at the prospect of hobbling along on those excruciating heels.

He raised his thick eyebrows.

"I mean, oh yes, I'd like that," I said.

Wincing, mincing in pain, I followed him down endless corridors.

"We'll call you," he said, dismissing me at last. "I have to warn you: We're flooded with applicants. But we'll let you know one way or other."

From a pay phone, I telephoned the employment agency, but the office had closed for the day, leaving me no choice but to teeter home in the borrowed shoes. On the way, I thought about how to get from the Lanes' front door down to the basement without drawing attention to my feet. I was not prepared to recount the degradation of being stripped of my own shoes in order to present myself for a job I knew in my heart that I had no hope of getting.

The minute I opened the door, I knew there was no escape. Matty was standing in the hallway. "Well, hi!" she said expectantly. I had told her that I was going to be out job hunting. "How did it go?"

"I'll come up and tell you in a minute," I said, hurrying past her as if between trains. "First I have to go to the bathroom."

I ran toward the basement like a geisha in haste. Halfway down the stairs, I slipped, clutched wildly at the bannister to try to break my fall, but ended up hurtling noisily and painfully to the bottom. It crossed my mind that I may have sprained my back and broken an ankle. But I was more concerned that Matty might run solicitously after me (and discover the shoes); so, shoes in hand, I hurried toward our room on all fours, noticing only when the door was safely shut behind me that one of the heels had been severed in the fall.

Still in the grip of irrational secrecy, I began to hammer the heel back into the shoe.

Shan got up from his bed and stood over me. "What the hell is going on?"

I pulled myself up onto the side of my bed, choking with hushed laughter, and spewed out the story bit by bit until we were both convulsed.

And when he tried to massage my swollen, inflamed ankle, it only tickled my funny bone and I kicked his hands away, unable to stop crying from laughing so hard.

After almost a year of increasing discomfort on everyone's part, we left the Lanes' at last and drove south in search of work in a warmer climate. In South Carolina, I found a job as a bank teller, hired to substitute for an employee on sick leave on the understanding that the job would last no more than three months. As it turned out, the bank kept me on for another three, but when that came to an end my brother and I set out on a drive to the Florida panhandle—a long drive that would bring me face-to-face with the changes in his behavior that shook me to the core.

We were headed for Pensacola, where in response to an ad for a second mate and factotum, Shan had been promised a berth on a Morgan Out Islander bound for the Bahamas. In the wheezing, fifteen-year-old Chrysler that the Lanes had signed over to us for a dollar (to spare them the trouble of junking it, they said), we started out with a kind of jollity that was nothing more than whistling in the dark. We were about to be separated for the first time in the year and a half since our arrival in America.

It wasn't long before our spirits began to sink, before the South of the Border signs turned stale and we fell silent under the numbing, hypnotic monotony of the highway. Waking from catnaps, I wished I could relieve him at the wheel, but I had never learned to drive. His eyes were bloodshot and bright with determination; his hands were a vise on the steering wheel. When we stopped for gas, he warned me under his breath that the thick accents of the attendants were put on to make fools of us.

Then, at a small town on the swampy outskirts of Pensacola, where we had to stop for repairs, I saw him approach the mechanic with baffling insincerity. After his mistrust of every stranger encountered on the way, I found his sudden friendliness difficult to fathom, and it was months before I understood the reason. It was at times most fraught with danger, when his fear had reached an all-consuming pitch, that he needed to outfox the stranger-enemy with sweet talk and subterfuge. He became ingenuous and fawning. And all the while he was secretly ill with fear.

Seeing his obsequiousness with the mechanic, I knew that he was caught in some spiraling confusion of fear and deceit, and I wanted to turn my back on the whole charade. In retrospect, I figure that he imputed to that mechanic all sorts of powers: the power to turn us down and leave us stranded in that spooky little tidewater town; the power to put a hex on the rest of our journey by tampering with the engine in sneaky ways; the power to exact from us any price he pleased, knowing we were easy marks.

I cringed to hear the false little attempts to win the mechanic over. "Sir," he said (and kept addressing him that way with almost every other sentence), "how is it, sir, that you know so much about cars?"

The mechanic, a burly, pot-bellied man with skin burned to a livid pink by the sun, was clearly not a talker. He grunted in answer, a sign (to me at least) that he couldn't take a question like that seriously.

But Shan was persistent. "You know, sir," he went on, "I always wanted to learn about cars; but it's not easy. People think it's all handwork and dirty work, but I think you have to be brainy to know about engines."

I couldn't bear to look at the mechanic, who was absorbed in wires underneath the open hood of the car. But then I heard Shan say, "We bought this car in another snake."

"Snake?" said the mechanic from under the hood.

"Yes, we drove it all the way from South Carolina. It's not a bad snake to live in. Pleasant weather. Better than most other snakes . . . "

"States," I said to the mechanic. "He means states."

"But I've heard good things about this snake, too," Shan continued, unbelievably.

I retreated into the car.

When we had paid the mechanic and were once more on the road, I said, "What was wrong with you just now? You kept saying 'snake' for 'state.'"

"It's the same thing," he said; "don't you get it? State, snake . . . poisonous bastards."

"You need to have your head examined," I said.

"Then you do, too," he said. "How is it you knew what I meant?" He was talking down at me from some unfamiliar plane of logic whose rules I would never understand.

"All right, then," I said, angrily, "do me a favor. Now that we are in a new snake, please try—"

"Snake?" he said, and laughed mockingly. "What snake? You mean state. You get your words all mixed up."

Now I was glad not to have to take the wheel. I was free to press my hands to my throbbing head and shut my eyes.

6

It was at the point when I was beginning to feel some mastery of life in America, when I had learned to drive a car and file a tax return, when I had found steady work and made acquaintances, when I could look around me and consider all the possibilities the new world had to offer—it was at this point, two years after our arrival in the States, that I was taken captive for the next two long years in which my brother fell apart.

In Pensacola, Shan had reported to the man with the yacht—the man who had hired him unseen. But after a week he had discovered that the promised cruise to the Bahamas was nothing more than bait to lure a boat lover to some seedy little marina in Pensacola, to work as maintenance man for less than minimum wage.

This, at any rate, was Shan's reason for quitting the job within a week—on the day, as it happened, that I had planned to return to South Carolina, in search of more permanent work. Now, both unemployed, we decided to stay on in Pensacola, where the motel I had checked into at least offered low monthly rates.

Within a week, fortuitously, I found work—again with a bank, and again only temporary. Meanwhile, for reasons I couldn't sort out, Shan had taken to hanging around the marina from which he had just resigned, having made peace with the man who had brought him there under false pretenses. Defending him, Shan said to me, "He's not a bad sort. He's quite a sailor. Man, he knows about sailing." And if it weren't for the bad business investment that was pushing him over the edge into bankruptcy, he would have offered Shan a decent salary. Really, he wasn't a bad sort.

"I feel sorry for the guy," Shan said. "I told him I'd help him out with his boats. He doesn't have to pay me."

In those days when I didn't know better, I was forever confronting my brother with what I thought was unassailable logic. He was jobless, we were broke; how could he afford to offer free services to a man who had cheated him in the first place? But he was always ready with an answer, a rebuttal, an intimation of hurt to deflect my ever-practical questions.

Then came the day when I thought the tide had turned: The boat owner had a friend who ran a small hotel in Vermont, and who was looking for someone willing to train as a cook. Shan was recommended, interviewed by telephone, and accepted. He left Pensacola high on renewed hopes of adventure and fortune, and in the next eight months I saw him only twice, which seemed a good sign. (By then I had moved to Chicago to take a promising, full-time job in the hope that I would be able to start night school in a year or so.) Meanwhile, Shan's long-distance calls reassured me that he was well paid, well settled, and reasonably content.

And so I was totally unprepared for the day when I got

home from work to find him sitting on the steps to my apartment. Surrounded by his bags, ragged, unshaven, pallid, he had never looked more like a refugee. And he had lost so much weight that I might not have known him on the street.

He seemed indifferent to my consternation, saying only that he had tired of the hotel in Vermont and had decided to hitchhike home. It was clear that pressing him with any questions would have been unrewarding at best. A week was to pass before he would bring up the subject—and then it was in a way that presaged for me his increasing breach with reality.

We were driving into town one afternoon when he started talking about Vermont: about how much he had enjoyed the air, the hills, the pines, even the snow. Something about his bland travelogue made me suspect that it was only the preamble to some unpleasant conclusion. I was right. He launched suddenly into an attack on the hotel where he had been working. The service was bad, the management was crooked, there were goings-on the likes of which he'd never seen.

"It's a frightful house," he said, lowering his voice, "and the guys in there are bad, bad guys."

"What do you mean *baaaad*?" I bleated, trying to tease him into precision.

"You're a bloody little idiot," he said.

"How so bad?" I asked, trying to sound contrite.

He said, "At first they were good to me."

"Who is they?"

"The guys I worked with in the kitchen. We slept in a dorm together. Six or seven or eight of us. They showed me how things worked and helped me out when I was stuck. We'd play cards at night, or go into town together on days off. Then things happened. They asked me to move into a different room, so they could have more space in the dorm.

Why didn't they ask one of their own kind to move? They asked me because I was the foreigner. I was different. I wasn't going to make trouble. So I moved. But I knew what they were doing. I'm not stupid. They were going to teach me a lesson."

"Why? What had you done? I thought you got along," I said, trying to follow his reasoning.

"They punish you for being different, don't you know that?" he said, as if I had been living in ignorance of a fundamental truth.

"I stayed quietly in my new room," he went on. "And then they started. At night, when I was asleep, they scratched at my door. When I went to open it, no one was there. When I would go back to sleep, the scratching would start again. I knew it was them. Once, they pounded on the door so hard, bang, bang, bang, bang, bang, I thought the door would break down. The minute I opened it, no one was there."

"Did you ask them about it? Didn't you say something?"

"Sure I said. I told them I knew what they were doing. I said, 'Why are you making life difficult for me? Why can't we be friends?' They pretended like they didn't know what I meant."

We were stopped by the light at an intersection, and I was trying to take in everything he had just told me when he said, quite matter-of-factly, "They raped me, you know."

The light turned green. I drove on mechanically, but my arms, my legs, my heart felt suddenly thick and heavy. It wasn't just the shock of his revelation, or the way he set off the explosive (coolly, almost challengingly). It was my own disbelief.

Up until then, I was prepared to accept his story. I knew that things did not necessarily happen the way he interpreted them. His distortions could turn the harmless word or look of a stranger into a dagger aimed straight at his heart.

It was possible, of course, that his roommates had baited him, and even scratched and pounded on his door. I didn't doubt he'd been genuinely upset. What froze me was that almost calculating mention of rape. I recognized it instantly, though inexplicably, as a lie. Furthermore, it was a lie told for effect. I could practically feel him holding his breath for my reaction.

In the shifting surges of anger and confusion, I could find no words. It might have struck me as odd that he, too, had nothing more to say, but by then I was in the clutch of a new kind of fear: I was not only afraid for my brother; I was afraid of him.

It was the beginning of a two-year sentence for us. We served it helplessly—he because there was no alternative, and I because his illness infected me with a great numbness that seemed to spread through flesh, bone, and spirit.

Once I had discovered my fear of him, it came to me that he feared me, too. It was different from his terror of the external world with its menacing strangers, portents, and events—a world in which the smallest things took on secret meaning, in which the man in the street harbored harmful thoughts and designs, in which passers-by talked about him in code, in which a coup in a remote land sent out a signal only he could understand.

The more he recoiled from these hazards, the more he needed to cling to me for protection and ballast. In the process, he conferred upon me such exaggerated strengths that I was turned into the mother of the child he had become.

He said to me once, "The earth is spinning too fast for me. One day I'm thrown here, another day I'm thrown there. I can't find my way back." And so I became the anchor to his unanchored self.

But at the same time that he fused himself to me, he

feared his dependency. And because I was the buffer between him and danger, I too moved in and out of the cast of characters that endangered his life. And one day, when he said to me, "I'm afraid for you, for the harm I might do you. The bad guys are inside me now," I took to sleeping behind a locked door at night.

It was always at night that he seemed to be worst. I would walk into the darkened living room and find him sitting in front of a blank television screen, intensely tuned in to some invisible, inaudible broadcast. It was at night that he paced the floor and kept me awake with the incessant, smacking sound of his fist pounding his thigh as if in answer to some terrible ache in his bones. And I would hear him sobbing as he lay on the daybed: "Oh, God, why am I crazy?"

A year had passed since his final return from Vermont —a year of sporadic but increasing breakdowns which I had tried in every way to repair on my own, with no lasting success. Yet I was incapable of seeking help.

Some sense of loyalty—narrow and simple-minded— imparted the idea that to turn my brother over to someone else would mean betrayal and abandonment. We had been in cahoots since childhood. I had kept his secrets, gone along with his stories and plans and dreams. The conspiracy had carried over from those days; and even now—when he was no longer the playmate and partner he had been; when he, by his own frightened admission, had been turned into a thing, a slave; when his suffering came not just from his illness, but from an awareness of it—even now the habit stayed.

It was easier to keep hoping that things would improve, to keep ministering to him the way I had as a child—when intuition told me that he was serving a death sentence of the mind. His past life had been among symbols he recognized and people who reflected the image of himself he wanted to see. His new life—stripped of his dreams, his beliefs, his supports—was a blank.

But the time came when I had to own up to my failings as my brother's keeper and healer. It was then—with the dark conscience and racing heart of an inexperienced criminal—that I secretly arranged to take him to a hospital.

But on the day itself, stricken by my arbitrariness, I tried to break the news to him, hoping against hope that persuasion might still be possible.

The dreadful scene went on for hours—through every extreme of his changing reactions. One minute he was agreeable; the next minute he was wild with fear. On and on it went: from suspicion and hatred to sudden lucidity; from self-recriminations over his illness to earnest, pleading vows to get well on his own. He cursed me and begged me. He even tried cunning—a pitifully transparent cunning.

When the doorbell rang to announce the arrival of the cab I had ordered, we both froze.

Then he got down on his knees, his hands clasped in frantic appeal, and implored me through a torrent of sobs and tears not to turn him in, not to put him away "with the real crazies."

"I'll get better on my own," he cried. "I swear I will. Maybe I've been pretending to be crazy just to shake everything and everyone up so the world will be all right. I'll stop that now. I'll be well. You'll see."

The bell rang and rang. Each time his arms tightened around my knees. From the waist down I had turned into stone, but my hands were free to tear at my hair, and my heart to continue its loud clapping. That sound! His uncontrolled sobbing was like the sound of some catastrophic eruption: an earthquake, a tidal wave, a boiling volcano.

When the bell had stopped and the cab had driven away, I pulled him up off the floor and led him to his daybed.

Exhaustion had calmed him down, but his body was seized with involuntary shudders. He turned to me with a last apology before falling asleep.

"The trouble is," he said, "I'm thinking about everything, and so I end up thinking about nothing."

Long after he was asleep, I sat by his bed, with no other solace than the unstable rhythm of his breath. It moved me to beg his forgiveness as abjectly as he had begged me not to turn him in.

From then on it was with resignation, with a sense of irremediable fate, that I chose to endure my undertaking. But it was a fate borne grudgingly, with hidden reproach. His spells and delusions often seemed to me absurd posturings; his flights of omnipotence, so wildly at odds with his devalued life, made me cringe; and even in his most cut-off moments, I began to feel an undertow of mockery.

I hated his necessary lies—his need to paint the world in colors grim enough to justify his own crumbling will. I hated his nostalgia for a past that never was, his view of the world we'd left behind as an idyll destroyed by the present. I hated his language of sentiment and triviality—a language of empty catchwords. He talked of old friends who gave him "love and respect," who had "made much of him"; he thanked me often for the gift of "a sister's love and affection." He disguised his mistrust of strangers by professing gratitude for the most trifling kindness or favor. ("Poor thing!" he would say of anyone who had shown him the merest courtesy. "What he did for me!"—as if kindness called for both gratitude and pity.)

Underneath all of my dutiful concern and care I raged at his illness, seeing it as nothing more than a breakdown of courage. I began to question not only the alleged heroics of his past—the heroics woven into the yarns he had charmed me with as a child; I began to doubt every fact of his life that I hadn't myself witnessed. He had held me to such pledges of secrecy that most of his stories had remained unverified.

Now I began to suspect his entire past. Whose word but his did I have that he had been born to a mad mountain woman? It was true that Father had taken him to be raised with the rebels in the hills and "toughened up" for the life of an insurgent's son; it was true that I had never seen my brother before the age of four. But who besides him had put the idea into my head that he was actually my half-brother, that he had had a mother other than my own? Had he invented this version as an ingenious way of denying Mother's death —a death too earth-shaking to absorb? Why else would his other, imagined mother, the mountain woman, have seemed to me, even as a child, so shadowy and unearthly a creature? Why else would she have simply disappeared one day, as Shan explained (offhandedly), during one of her deranged wanderings?

Which of his stories, then, could be held to account? Was Father's cruelty as extreme as he had made it out to be? Or was Shan predisposed from his earliest imaginings to give to Father—and all larger, stronger beings—a brute shape, a murderous intent?

In these and all other accruing suspicions, I was becoming as ungrounded in my beliefs as was he. I prided myself that while he was losing touch with the real things of the earth, I was confronting them solidly. His lack of courage led me into foolhardy displays of brazenness that I mistook for bravery. I walked the streets at unsafe hours; in the bus, at street crossings, in the grocery store, I stood my ground, defiantly, at the hint of the pettiest slight or challenge. His lapses into sentimentality brought out in me a need to avoid it at all costs, to fix on reality a hard, unblinking eye.

I began to see his sickness as an outgrowth of both weakness and stupidity. It was weak and stupid of him not to be able to find a way out of his predicament.

And all the while I myself could not see beyond the

ground in front of my nose. I was busy nursing an invalid
—while perpetuating his illness without knowing it.

I had sedated myself on drudgery, on a daily routine in
which all concern boiled down to waking up in time to
prepare our meals for the day before setting out for work,
and returning home to eat and clean up. Food came to be
the sum and substance of our days. When silence loomed,
we could always turn to a discussion of the day's menu: what
we would eat for the next meal, how it should be prepared,
what it should taste like, and the satisfaction it would bring.
In time, all my aspirations seemed to revolve around the pot
on the stove, on the amount of food I could get him to eat.
To compensate for the stinginess of my affection, I indulged
him in his simpler cravings. I fed him all the starch and
grease he wanted: mounds of glutenous rice swimming in
oily stews; lumps of fatty pork fried in batter; unlimited
helpings of ice cream; sodas, potato chips, and candy bars.

The weight and leaden apathy he gained as a result only
vindicated the revulsion that lay behind my care. I noted the
discharge at the corners of his eyes, the untended hair, the
greasy skin, the slackness of his body with its metallic smell
—and felt a disgust that all my powers of charity could not
contain.

How was it bearable? I think even now. The clocks must
have run differently then; they must have bent time to make
endurance possible—in the same merciful way that the occasional absurdity would rear its distracting head.

I remember one giddy afternoon when, more broke than
usual, we wandered through a giant grocery store, wheeling
two carts which we filled indiscriminately with every expensive item we fancied: cheeses and meats, caviar and
canned asparagus, jams and teas, melons and berries, and
cakes and pies. When the carts were full, we left them in the
aisles, walked out of the store, and ended the fantasy empty-
handed, feeling poorer and hungrier than ever.

This happened in one of his good periods, in a rare burst of frivolity when he could actually lose himself in some sport without looking over his shoulder. The rest of the time he was locked into his secret logic, unable to disregard the extraneous, to sit back and laugh at the world.

Passing an industrial trash can on a street one day, he turned around and came back to read the sign on it: PLACE ON AN EVEN SURFACE. DO NOT PLAY IN AND AROUND TRASH CAN.

"What's the matter?" I asked, as he stood poring over the sign.

"It's really instructions for two guys," he said. "I mean, the guy who places the trash can on an even surface isn't the same guy who's going to be playing in it."

I didn't know whether to laugh or to cry. Was there possibly hope for recovery? Maybe I would come home one day to find him grounded solidly in the world once more.

But then, without a moment's notice, he could withdraw into his fortress where he saw and heard things hidden from me. Sometimes I could pick up the signals marking his retreats: a straight-backed posture when he took a seat, a tightening grip on the arms of his chair, a restless foot-tapping, an inability to look me in the eye.

Wishes began to take fleeting shape in my thoughts—wishes that his life might come to an end. At night, in my dreams, I saw him killed in a traffic accident that left me picking up the severed limbs of his body; I saw him limping across a long bridge on a starless night, dripping with blood from some violent injury, yet singing a cheerful calypso before lowering himself into the black waters below the bridge—which became the waters of our lake back home.

By day, I made amends for my murderous dreams with attempts at rehabilitation. I scanned the want ads in search of that one small untaxing job which might magically turn into the lifeline leading out of his darkness.

It didn't surprise me that on the morning of a job interview—the first in several months that I had been able to prod him into—he complained of a vague indigestion. I was familiar with his phobia about work and suspected him at once of malingering. Because I had gone to some lengths to set up his appointment and arranged to be picked up for work so that he would have the car, I left the house abruptly, with the minimum of sympathy for his sudden malaise.

But I came home that afternoon to find a note on the dining table: I WENT TO THE INTERVIEW AFTER ALL. GOODBYE, SHAN. There had been few occasions that required his leaving me notes, but I couldn't recall having seen the same salutation. The GOODBYE set off an alarm in me so that I was more than relieved to see him walk through the door. I started to ask him about the interview, but stopped when I saw the state he was in. He looked pinched with fatigue. "God, I feel lousy," he said, throwing the car keys on the table and himself on the daybed. "My stomach is really paining me."

"Hurting me," I corrected him, ridiculously; but he was in no condition to notice. He was doubled up in pain, and sweating.

"What did you eat for lunch?" I asked.

"Nothing," he said. "My stomach was sour."

"No wonder you feel bad," I said, and went into the kitchen to prepare his meal.

He ate with his usual ravenous speed, but without relish. "Chew your food," I said. "You'll only feel worse otherwise."

The meal seemed to settle his stomach. He moved into the living room and collapsed into a chair, sighing with relief to be rid of the pain. I cleared the table and rinsed the dishes in the kitchen sink. The phone rang; I went into the living room to answer it. Wrong number. A few seconds later it rang again. I called out to Shan from the kitchen to ignore it, but he had already crossed the room to pick up the telephone.

When I came out of the kitchen, he still had the receiver in his hand, but it hung limply at his side. He wore such an expression of shock that I thought the bad news had come with the phone call, but in the next moment he had let go of the receiver and was beating his chest with groans of pain. I stood helplessly by the daybed. "Come and lie down here," was all I could say. He started toward me, both hands pressed to his heart, but halfway across the room he fell— first on his knees, and then on his side. By the time he hit the ground, he was perfectly still.

Later, when the emergency medical team had arrived, when they had cleared the furniture around him and were trying to bring him back to life, I was not there to watch or take part. I was biding my time behind the closed door to my room, my hands pressed over my ears to shut out any hint of a sentence pronounced by the voices outside. I wanted only to remain apart from the chaos that churned on the other side of the door, to hide the way I had hidden when, as a child, I had been invited by one of the maids to witness the birth of a litter of kittens. The spectacle of birth had been too awesome for me to bear, and I had fled to my room in panic. Now I wanted to flee from death as I had fled from birth, to escape from those terrors beyond my control.

I remained in my room until they had taken him away. But I knew, long before he had reached the hospital, that my despairing dreams had come to pass.

PART TWO

7

When they wheeled me into Intensive Care, the pain had shifted to the backs of my eyes, which seemed to be glued shut. I badly wanted to pry my lids apart, but both arms had been strapped to my sides. Some hazy instinct directed me to relax the frown of tension around my aching eyes; and in that moment I discovered the source of the irritation.

I had been standing in front of a high-rise building. The façade was of cut glass, blinding in its intricacy. Shielding my eyes from the glare, I went inside. At once the pain disappeared.

The walls on the inside were also made of glass, but glass with the smooth, oily sheen of pearls. I walked through silent, cavernous rooms and came across groups of mannequins posing in various attitudes of work and play. An innocent tableau—but the figures, on closer inspection, seemed aloof and alien, not at all what they appeared to be. I began to look very closely, even reaching out to touch one of them. To my amazement, I discovered that it had been crafted out of fine rice paper and folded like origami.

A plaque beneath a group of these figures—a plaque such as one sees in museums—informed me that the rice paper was an amalgam of ground glass and a carbon extract from the subterranean remains of a bygone civilization.

I stood back to study these curious artifacts. From afar, they took on the appearance of smoke-colored glass; up close they sparkled and sent out prisms in colors too blinding to be distinguished.

I stopped to read another plaque. It said: "Through the action of carbon on glass, light is trapped and returned in the angles and points of the paper in such a way as to reflect each figure's innermost qualities."

So that's how it was to stumble upon the interiority of human beings! I paused to look at an infant, or what had once been an infant, and saw unfolding before me its very dreams at the moment of birth.

Then I happened to glance out a window. Stretching out into an infinite horizon was a vast tundra, iced over and untouched by the merest breath of wind. Here and there, the snowy expanse was dotted with forlorn scarecrows that kept a petrified vigil.

I started down a steep flight of stairs and was suddenly racked by a whirlwind created by the furor of ghosts that had been trapped in the stairwell.

This is dangerous, I thought. I must warn the others. But when I looked around, the figures had vanished. The glassy hallways were now deserted.

I felt a prisoner from the time they wheeled me in and kept me waiting in the empty office while I watched them go through my bag and remove nail clippers, pocket scissors, needle, and thread (Why the thread? I wondered).

Their smiles made a plea for understanding: the precaution was in my best interests. I knew it was as much for themselves as for me, but I returned the smiles. I wanted to present myself, despite the evidence, as a reasonable human being.

I felt the imprisonment throughout the endless questions and examinations and forms. I felt it increasingly as I saw the rules pinned to the wall: "The policy of the unit is to keep the door unlocked during the day. The door will be locked routinely at 11:30 P.M. However, there may be other times when the staff feel that, in order to best meet the needs of the community, the door should be locked."

And when they wheeled me down the hall to my room, the signs on the doors ("BATH," "OFFICE," "SUPPLIES") triggered worse suspicions. It was the quotation marks on the signs that alarmed me. I took those marks to signify euphemisms. Surely some barbaric form of hydropathy went on behind the room marked "BATH." Surely the "OFFICE" was there for the third degree, and "SUPPLIES" for storing the intruments of torture.

The hysteria passed; behind those doors I discovered in time nothing but an ordinary bathroom, an ordinary office, an ordinary roomful of supplies.

But I was still a prisoner.

I dreamed of going home just once, just long enough to collect a comb, a book, a jar of lemon pickles, a pair of scissors. (In my new surroundings I needed a permit even for the temporary use of any arts-and-crafts instrument: crochet needle, chisel, gouge, or string.) I longed to be out in the open.

It was early April and spring was in sudden bloom, but from behind the plate glass at the end of the hall, I saw only a flat rendition of the new season. Cardinals flitted through the holly trees; the azaleas shook in the wind; the sky was bright and only faintly smudged with cloud. Farther down, the foreshortened highway swept past the building, carrying its quick current of cars. Beyond it, about a mile away, the ground rose sharply to a low white fence enclosing a trio of horses that moved about in slow motion.

But it was all just a picture—a moving picture on a screen. I could have poked my finger through the entire insubstantial image.

Were they already expecting me on the ward, or was it only a self-important fantasy that made it seem as if they all knew who I was and what I had done the moment I stood at the door? The scene was so homey and companionable that I wondered if it had been staged solely to put me at ease.

Sarah was kneading dough at the end of the long dining table, surrounded by buttered baking pans. The room was fragrant with cardamom and yeast. The television was turned on to a soundless soap opera. Jolene had pulled up a stool close to the set and was smiling down at the screen, one hand on the set as though it needed affection on top of attention. Helga and Maria were sitting knee-to-knee, in quiet conversation. Brian was bent over a game of Scrabble with one of the attendants, at the opposite end of the table from Sarah. Paddy was strumming on his guitar and singing in a thick, hoarse voice, "*A lesson too late for the learning . . . made of sand, made of sand . . .* " Winston sat listening, arms folded, eyes closed.

It was Winston who rose to greet me first, shaking my hand with grave diplomacy. I smelled peppermint on his breath. He turned to introduce me to the others and was interrupted by Helga's greeting—a soft mumble that acted as insurance against rebuff. "Velcome, velcome," she said in a voice that was prepared to assume the pretense of talking to herself. "Soon vill be breakfast and then a little bit ve put our heads together to discuss what for snacks ve should order tomorrow. Always ve are meeting . . . " and she fell asleep in mid-sentence, her short pink arms settling comfortably across the lumpy expanse of her breast, belly, and lap. Maria gave me a timid and apologetic smile, as if she were responsible for Helga's lapse.

"Just watch," said Sarah, not to anyone in particular. "The minute she smells food, she'll snap out of her sleep."

Breakfast arrived on a trolley of stacked trays, and true to Sarah's prediction, Helga sat up expectantly. Then, seeing she was the focus of amused observation, she frowned, sighed, and pretended to yawn. While the trays were being set on the table she began to pace the floor, and in the end reached into the cabinet above the stove. There she reached into a paper bag for a handful of chocolate-chip cookies and stuffed them into her mouth, urgently. Still frowning, she took her place at the table and began to talk to her tray of food. "I must eat well, *sonst* I shall feel veak all day. Narcolepsy is a serious illness, one needs food. Winston, are you not eating your roll today? You should eat it, it's good for you." Before Winston could answer, she reached for his roll and tore it in half. "Ach, Robin!" she said through a full mouth. "How vos the run?"

A very young girl with cropped ash-blond hair and a boy's frame had just come in. "Nine miles," she said. She was sweating heavily.

"Robin, what is this?" Helga said, pointing to a plastic cup of grapefruit sections. "You are leaving your dessert again? Such a vaste! No, I shall take it. One shouldn't vaste."

Robin seemed about to protest, but smiled and said nothing.

"Helga," said Sarah, "you really ought to go on a thousand-calorie diet, you know."

"Vot?" Helga looked as shocked as if the death of a close friend had just been announced.

"Yes. Melt away all that blubber. Could feed an army of Eskimos with it."

"Sarah, vot are you talking? Do you not understand that

I need this food to give me strength? Narcolepsy is veaken-ing, believe me."

"Helga, Helga," said Sarah, setting down her fork with exaggerated care. "You and your bloody narcolepsy. You know what I think? I don't think you have narcolepsy at all. I think you fall asleep in the middle of what you're saying because you like to tune out whenever you want. You talk, talk, talk at people, run your mouth off without ever listen-ing, because you can't handle things when the going gets rough. You can't bear to face facts, you can't bear to see yourself as you really are. Pitiful."

"Enough, enough!" shrieked Helga. "I heff hed enough. Firsht is my veight, zen my narcolepsy. I can't take it any-more!" She fled the room in a fast waddle.

Sarah began to butter a roll. "Boy, is she touchy!"

Brian got up from his seat and lit a cigarette. He was licking his lips and trying to smile at the same time.

"Sarah, I think that was unnecessarily cruel."

Through a mouthful of bread, Sarah replied, "Maybe, maybe not."

"I mean, we're all trying to help each other in a con-structive way."

Sarah leaned across the table. "Paddy, I see you're not eating your bacon. Can I have it?"

Paddy picked up a piece of bacon from his tray and threw it with a flourish across the table. It landed squarely on Winston's omelette.

"Paddy, man," said Winston, looking quite sad, "you do that one more time and I'll kill you." He removed the bacon with the tips of his fingernails and got up to wash his hands.

"Brian," said Sarah, "I wish you'd stop being so uptight, you know. I mean, it can get on a person's nerves. You just *cannot* sit still. Always shaking your leg and licking your lips. Relax."

Brian looked around the room with grim satisfaction, as

if he had been expecting just such an attack. "I lick my lips because my mouth is dry from the medication."

"Bullshit. You lick your lips because it's a nervous tic. And you defend Helga because you think you're still in the public defender's office. What a legal beagle, with all your fairness and on-the-one-hand, on-the-other-hand crap."

Brian smiled indulgently.

"That's right," continued Sarah. "Turn the other cheek." In a throaty bass, she sang, "*How do I know? The Bible tells me so,*" and rolled her eyes toward the ceiling. "You God-fearing people have to stick together. You and your revelations and messages from God. Helga and her auras. Her mystic auras. Or *owras* as she calls them. What a pair."

"Sarah, do you mind?" Winston broke in. "I've got a terrible headache."

"Winston, you're a hypochondriac," she said, and blew him a kiss. As she cleared her tray, she turned to me. "It's a madhouse, what can I say? But you'll get used to it."

Twice a day we met to lay our inner selves out on the dissecting table, while the group offered sympathy, diagnosis, and prescription. In the words of the official handbook distributed to all who entered 3 East: "This is a setting where staff and community members are together in a group for the good of each individual's recovery."

But in the months that followed, the community spirit failed me often and without warning. After weeks of repetitious discussions about Winston's compulsion to brush his teeth a dozen times a day, I suffered a lapse and said something about his brushing his boots, when I meant to say his teeth.

Instantly, the onus was on me to explain so curious a slip of the tongue. Tired of this microscopic scrutiny of our every thought, every motive, every sentiment, I wanted only to remain silent. But I had learned about the significance that could attach to a refusal to speak. So I admitted in the end that Winston's endless toothbrushing had reminded me of a book I had picked up in the reading room that day. It was a collection of love letters between a poet and a married woman.

She had written to him complaining about some aspect of her unhappy marriage. In reply, her lover wrote: "You pour the whole . . . inexhaustible secret . . . again and again, into the worry over his boots. Something in it torments me, I don't know exactly what. . . . Should you leave him he will either live with another woman or go and live in a boarding-house, and his boots will be better cleaned than now . . ." Later, in response to more agonizing over her husband's boots, he wrote again: "Oh, knowledge of human nature! What should I have against your polishing the boots so beautifully! Polish them beautifully by all means, then put them into a corner and let the thing be done with. It's only that you polish them in your mind all day long; this torments me sometimes (and does not clean the boots)."

I confessed that I felt about Winston's teeth something like what the man had felt for those troublesome boots; that I had been saying to myself: "Polish them, Winston, if you must, polish them beautifully by all means, I have nothing against your polishing your teeth all day."

I saw Kim, one of the social workers, exchange glances with a nurse. It always surprised me that the staff was not better trained to conceal suspicion or prejudice. Kim cleared her throat and wondered aloud about my need to approach a feeling through literary anecdote. She wondered if such an indirect expression wasn't simply a safe way of telling Winston off for taking center stage.

I answered with silence and my best effort at what the staff called "a flat affect," but later that day Kim came to catechize me on my hostility. She was standing too close for comfort, obliging me to study the pores on her oily nose. She reminded me of someone, but for a while I couldn't think who.

"What hostility?" I said. And then I remembered: She looked just like Mother Immaculata.

I was taken back to the time when I was waking up to the meanings and shadings of ordinary words, when a word like "love" gave off a lambency that warmed me to the deeps. "Love" leaped out at me from the pages of books and the phrases of songs. I wrote it out experimentally, as one practices a signature, in my notebooks, on the canted surface of my desk, or while idly scratching with a stick in the ground. It inspired the composition of letters to an as yet unknown object of devotion.

"My dearest love," the letters began. "It is you in the entire universe that I love. I love you with all the power of the sun and all the sweetness of the moon. I would die for you. I would cut off my arms and legs. With all my love . . ."

The letters piled up in my desk until Mother Immaculata discovered them during one of her surprise raids.

She waited for an audience; only when the classroom was full did she call me to the front, rocking on her heels with unconcealed relish. She had the letters rolled into a cylinder and was smacking the palm of one hand with it, marking time to an attack from which there was no retreat.

"Tell me the truth and you won't be sorry," she said. How well I knew that tone: so seductive and fraught with entrapment. "Who is this person you are writing to?"

"No one, Mother." An itch began to break out across my face.

"You know you'll be sorry if you lie."

I stood a better chance of acquittal if I looked her in the eye, but holding her gaze was not easy. She wore glasses as thick and dim as unwashed windows, and behind them her eyes were as shifty as a crustacean's.

"I'm not lying, Mother. I swear upon God."

"How dare you swear! Don't you know it's a sin?" Her face had taken on the color of boiled crayfish. At that moment, she wasn't the "white monkey" that the girls used to call the Irish nuns behind their backs. She was moist with anger. Sweat formed on her forehead, her nose, and her upper lip, matting the pale mustache.

"I'm sorry, Mother."

She blew out her cheeks, trying hard to regain composure. Her breath struck me full in the face. It was like a whiff of river air, cold, fishy, and sour. "Now tell me who the letters are for."

The itch had settled at the corners of my mouth and was pulling my lips down in an uncontrollable tremor. "I wrote them for fun. Not for anyone."

Mother Immaculata raised her arms and the long white sleeves of her robe fell back, releasing a smell of sweat and starch. She took me by the shoulders and shook me steadily and hard, as if she could dislodge the truth from me in that way. All the while she was reciting through clenched teeth, like a jingle, "Eleven years old and writing this smut?!"

Revenge consumed me for months. Someday I would humiliate her as she had humiliated me. I would catch her without her veil, then throw back my head and howl at her bald pate.

I waited for the chance at our annual three-day retreat, when those of us ordinarily lucky enough to be day students had to swallow a taste of boarding life under the nuns. During the rest period in the hot muggy afternoons, still reeling from the rosaries, confessions, and sermons that glorified punishment and gore, I settled down in the library, pretending to be absorbed in the stained, mildewed books on the lives of the saints, but dreaming instead of my revenge.

This bloodthirst for a glimpse of a bald-headed nun was a common preoccupation. At night, when the rustlings in the nuns' rooms had died down, some of the girls would try to smoke them out by rolling marbles down the dorm or hurling a shoe across the floor. But no matter how quickly the nuns appeared, their heads were always covered.

Our luck turned late one night, when one of the girls, a diabetic, fell out of bed in a seizure. Shrill voices sounded the alarm. Mother Immaculata flew out of her room in a long housecoat. *Mirabile visu!* Her head was bare!

But as she knelt down to minister to the unconscious girl, the lights went on and I saw with a shock that her head, far from being shaven, was covered with coppery curls that shone in the harsh overhead fluorescent light. Her cheeks were smooth and rosy; she could have been the model for one of those simpering, fat-faced *putti* that frolicked in the nave of our chapel.

Revenge was not always sweet.

During those daily reports at 3 East, we all had our escapes. Helga nodded off at moments when the emotional current ran high. Maria excused herself abruptly to attend to her migraines. Winston had perfected the knack of tapping his foot while he dozed.

Once, when Sarah was recounting a long, dull dream, he leaned back in his chair, closed his eyes as if to concentrate, and began tapping his foot so as to nap undetected. But toward the end, Sarah's dream took an unexpected turn, involving a cat that laid five eggs—which then turned into human infants.

"My mother had left the eggs out on the leaves," she said. "I couldn't believe anyone could be so callous. So I put the eggs, I mean the babies, into a basket and brought them inside."

Winston woke up at this point. Eager to appear as if he

had been alert all along, he turned to Sarah. "You're putting me on," he said. "A cat laid eggs? You must have dreamed all that stuff."

Startled by our laughter, he cast about the room to direct the focus away from himself, saying, "Now who would like to continue with his report?" Embarrassment made him sound like the leader he wasn't.

Sarah leaned toward Jolene and whispered. Jolene broke out in a wide smile. Her smile seemed to affect her whole body: Her eyes grew moist; her nostrils quivered; her teeth shone; dimples played on her chin and cheeks. She crossed and recrossed her massive, mahogany-colored arms and legs.

"I think Jolene has something to say," Sarah said.

Jolene looked down at her slippers, sighed heftily, and began:

"All right, honey, I'll say it. Everybody here . . . I just want to say everybody here been saying I's so quiet, Jolene's so quiet, just as quiet's can be; why you don't speak up, Jolene? So I reckon I'll say a couple of things been on my mind. I just want to say I been so happy here, everybody been treating me so kind, reading me picture books and" (she held up a children's book called *The Beaneaters*) "some of you even learned me to read a little. My mama—God rest her soul—never could read no book. She be blind. Blind as a bat. But never had trouble knowing where things were. Now all you people here so nice and friendly I just want to say how much I 'preciate."

She looked around the room, nodding her thanks here and there, smiling. Sarah reached out for her hand and squeezed it. "Right on, Jolene, I think it's great what you just said."

"And I just want to say," Jolene began again, propelled by new confidence, "my dreams ain't so bad no more. Do you all remember when it seemed like every single night I be dreaming about that baby in my sleep and its head keep falling off and I try and try to stick it back on with jelly? And those chickens with heads like people? And those voices? Well. It ain't so bad no more. Maybe even those voices go away soon. Maybe they stop telling me to tear myself up and scratch my skin till blood come out. Everybody been so nice to me.

"But I'll tell you one more thing," she said, as though remembering an incident of long ago. "I ain't thinking of marriage. My uncle, the man who come visit me here? You seen him around, a good-lookin' man? Well, he ain't really an uncle. It's just what I call him. He say maybe I should think of marriage when I'm well; maybe a man in my bed shut those voices up good. But I tell him sex is sex and what I hear is what I hear. That's all he wants, my uncle. And when I don't give, boy, he sure gets mad. Yes, sir. One time"—she giggled—"one time he be so mad at me, he say, Jolene, girl, what you know about sex when you ain't never sucked no dick? And I says to him, Uncle, maybe I ain't never sucked no dick and maybe I never will, but let me tell you I's a woman and ain't no woman around don't know what sex is. Yes, sir, everybody here been so nice to me. I just wanted to say a few words."

These group sessions brought out a confusion caused by both a lack of freedom and an excess of it. Within the locked entrances at either end of the hall, we were free to pry open the trapdoors to memory and feeling, to descend into the unknowns of ourselves. We were no longer in the actual world, where life has to be consumed in safe doses and where what cannot be digested must not be bitten off.

We were free to test out a new kind of freedom—and we did so in startlingly similar ways.

The tears, the outbursts, the unsettling revelations that we could indulge in with impunity all exposed our yearning to be children again. After all we had been through to gain that costly freedom from sanity's pretenses, we were drawn, it seemed, only to the memories and acts of child-hood.

Our Groups often turned into play groups, where we reveled in kindergarten chaos. This struck me on my very first day on the ward, when the therapist arrived in her leotard and Pakistani skirt to take us through the motions of occupational therapy.

"Today," she said, when we were all seated in a circle, "I want to ask each of you to use your body to say whatever you're feeling at the moment." She demonstrated by shaking her arms and legs as though to air out her bones.

I took my cue from the others. Robin was swaying dreamily in her seat. Paddy was beating on an imaginary drum and nodding to a private rhythm. Maria made a dainty hand-wringing gesture. Brian, aping Robin, swayed—but uneasily. Jolene was shaking with quiet laughter. Helga, frowning, had drawn her chair away from the circle, saying, "Ach, mensch. This I cannot do. This foolishness. I heff a serious illness. Narcolepsy. Vot has this foolishness to do mit narcolepsy?"

I did my bit with a form of stretching exercise.

In a corner of the room, away from the circle, Sarah was sitting immobile. The therapist, still doing the skeleton's dance, said, "Sarah isn't participating. That, too, is a form of self-expression. She's saying something by just sitting there. What could you be saying, Sarah?"

"That," said Sarah, addressing the wall, "is for me to know and for you to find out."

"You seem to be expressing some hostility, Sarah. You seem to have a lot of it these days."

Sarah turned around and considered the loose-limbed therapist. "And you seem to be expressing some idiocy. You seem to have a lot of it."

The therapist turned to us with a look that was meant to appoint us her witnesses, then got up from her chair and walked to the table at the back of the room. She had a dancer's splayed feet and jaunty walk. "Let's have a little music," she said, searching through a stack of records. "Now, what would everyone like to hear?"

"Everyone doesn't want to hear the same thing, for God's sake," said Sarah. "It isn't like we all have one ear, one brain. I don't know what everyone wants to hear, but I know what I want to hear."

"Sarah, for pity's sake," said Winston, who had just come into the room, "why does it always have to be *that*? It's about time we had something different."

"Yeah? Like what, Win-ston?" said Sarah. She sang his name with a heavy stress on the *ston*.

"Like Elton *John*," said Winston, using the same intonation.

"Elton John sucks," said Sarah.

"Sarah," Winston said, smiling in his sleepy-eyed way and patting his helmet of tight curls, "you're a gentleman and a scholar; but your taste in music leaves something to be desired."

"All right, all right," the therapist cut in, sighing and touching her temples with the tips of her fingers. "Let's forget the music for a while. Let's do this little exercise. Now, this is a beach ball I've just filled."

"With hot air," said Sarah.

"I thought we would use it," said the therapist, maintaining her smile, "to express our feelings for each other, by passing it around—by the way we pass it around from one to another. Shall we try?"

She offered the ball to Brian, who was sitting next to her, as though it were a plate of appetizers. Brian licked his lips, accepted it tentatively, and threw it to Robin who dropped it and looked crushed. Paddy picked it up, lifted it to his face, and kissed it tenderly. Then, unexpectedly, he gave the ball a swipe in Helga's direction, startling her out of sleep.

"Vot, vot?" she said, alarmed, as the ball hit her lap. Then she dozed off again.

"Helga!" said the therapist sharply. "Are you with us? We are passing the ball around."

"Sorry, sorry," said Helga, straightening her back and folding her arms with renewed resolve.

Maria picked up the ball with a coy little smile (a gesture more in keeping with the retrieval of an undergarment in public) and pushed it gently toward Sarah, who had been waiting impatiently for her turn. She pounced on the ball and sat on it briefly, giggling, before sliding off the ball and the chair. Winston reached out to stop it from rolling across the room and bounced it off Sarah's head. Hiccoughing with laughter, Sarah hurled the ball back at him. Paddy intercepted it and threw it to Winston, who tucked it under his arm and began sprinting around the room, while Sarah, hair flying, face aflame, gave chase. She tackled him with a leap onto his back and clung to his neck until he lost his balance and fell onto Helga, who collapsed, chair and all, with heavy breathing and squeals of distress. "Stop it, I tell you, stop it. Please, I am a sick woman. Please. This is for me too dangerous."

"Oh, Helga, let me help you, you poor thing," said Sarah, choking on her laughter. She began tugging at Helga's squat arms, but fell instead onto the floor beside her, where she lay on her back, kicking her legs and howling, "What a madhouse!"

Once, when we were gathered to play charades, Robin got up to take her turn and drew *The Sound and the Fury*. We could see her dread—even before someone on the opposing team said thoughtlessly, "Easy! Oh, easy!"

In the exercise room, I often paused in the midst of my halfhearted calisthenics to watch Robin. She could pound the treadmill for an hour at a time, her eyes fixed ahead, blind to the traffic of convalescents in wheelchairs who pulled themselves along the railings beneath her.

The treadmill ran on a platform above the other gadgets and contraptions of the exercise room, and on that short, interminable stretch of track Robin seemed caught in weightless, mindless, effortless motion, directed by a spell and forever doomed to run.

Her face shone with sweat but otherwise showed little stress. It was a small, smooth face, and with her cap of ragged hair and her flat, stringy body she could have been a young boy. But she had a pinched, suspicious expression, and her body seemed stripped of all sexuality so that it was really neither girlish nor boyish, but simply an efficient human form moving along in tireless precision.

As she sprinted in place, almost disembodied in her coordination, I could see the marks of self-inflicted injury—the roadmap of scars on the insides of her wrists, the potholes along her arms left by cigarette burns.

Now, in the midst of charades, it was hard to believe that the slight, limp figure in the middle of the room was capable of long-distance running, or of any act of determination. Her face, her body, her gestures seemed to shrink as she stared at the scrap of paper in her hand. "I can't," she said, almost inaudibly. "I just can't."

Try, try! we urged. *Take it easy. What is it? Book? Movie? Song? How many words, how many syllables? What does it sound like? What does it rhyme with?*

"I can't do it," she repeated. "I don't know how."

"Robin, for God's sake, just try. All you have to do is try," Winston pleaded.

But Robin stood frozen in the middle of the circle. It was unbearable to sit and watch her any longer—her pinched face, her disfigured wrists—so I rose and offered to take her place. And drew *Tristan and Isolde*.

I began. *Three words. The second word is small*.

"The?" "Of?" "And?"

Yes. And. And. I stopped them.

The first word, I continued, and pretended to sneeze.

"Sneeze?" said someone. I shook my head, sneezed again, blew my nose.

"Cold?"

Yes, yes, I nodded. I curled my forefinger into my thumb to describe a tiny circle: *A pill, to be taken,* I demonstrated.

"Medicine?" said someone. "Drugs? A pill?"

I sneezed again.

"A cold pill?" said someone.

Yes, yes! I nodded. *Keep going.*

"Cold pill? Contac?"

Close, close! I nodded.

"Like Contac?"

Yes.

"Sinutab?"

No.

"Dristan?"

That's it! I jumped.

"Dristan . . . and . . ."

"Tristan and Isolde!" Brian shouted.

Winston looked at his watch. "Forty-five seconds!"

Applause.

I went back to my seat followed by Robin's penetrating stare. From across the room I saw her face closing in on itself with mistrust. Her look accused me of perfidy worse than a mere showing off at her expense. Later, she said to me in passing, "Why are you really here? You're not like the rest of us; your past is so different; yet you know your way around." It was an accusation, not a question.

One day she came into the living room when Paddy and I were alone. He was busy with his guitar, alternately riffling through chords and scribbling hieroglyphs in his notebook; and I was watching him.

"Robin! Hey!" he said cheerfully. "Why do you want to die?"

Robin turned her back to us. I saw it stiffen before she left the room.

"Why do you want to live?" I said to Paddy. The question came out harsher than I had intended. "I mean," I said, "the same questions you ask about dying can also be asked about living."

Paddy looked at me with sudden interest. "You remind me of an otter," he said.

"Why an otter?"

"Because of the stripe down your back."

Instinctively, I reached around to feel my back.

"This stripe," I said. "Do you have one, too?"

"Sure. See for yourself." He set down the guitar and took off his shirt, revealing a narrow, childlike chest. He turned his back to me and fingered the chain link of verte-brae. "That's my stripe," he said. "Meditate, and you can see anything. That's what I do: I meditate *and* medicate."

I was just getting the hang of his language and so I said, "Are beavers related to lemmings?"

"I think so," he replied. "Anyway, we all live to become comrades in death."

Then, abruptly, the game came to an end. "Oh, you gyp-sy con-artist, you—getting me to play my guitar," he said, as though I had enticed him into the most illicit of schemes.

He returned to his guitar and strummed loudly, a sign that he was tired of talk. He was shutting me out because I had been duped into humoring him. The signal sent a shiver of recognition through me. Shan had done that sort of thing with some regularity. The crosscurrents of his ill-ness would suck me into a swirl of complicity one minute, and in the next cast me out for allowing myself to be snared. How I felt the punishment of my narrow sanity.

8

My brother's village sat in cloud country, high on the shoulder of a mountain ledge. Beyond acres of mist lay the Great Snow Range, cloaked for most of the year in milky shadow. The air carried sounds of glacial grindings and shearings where the long rivers of the continent began their southward, eastward, or northward plunges.

Mist billowed over the twenty-hut village, opening now and then to reveal the glint of a crooked needle in the gorges below. There, in the cold dark currents of the jade river, crocodiles slid over the bedrock and edelweiss foamed on the sheer sides of the gorge. The water was sea green, colored, they said, by a floor of solid jade. But the legendary treasure remained untouched, protected by the river spirit and a slump in the mining industry following government control.

In Grandfather's time, fortunes were made on the banks

of that river. With crowbars, shovels, and spades, the villagers would pit the earth with jade mines for a bowl of rice, a sprinkling of salt fish, and the promise of half the spoils held out by lowland prospectors who provided the instruments and sat back to watch the villagers do the rest.

By the time Shan was born the trade routes had shifted, starting farther up, in the poppy fields along the ravines of the borderland rain forests, and making their way down the slippery hills to morphine refineries in the south. The trade was new but the routes were ancient: mountain trails that had been cut over the centuries by smugglers, traders, and farmers in search of new fields, all leading mules that hadn't yet succumbed to diseases like *surra*.

Now it was the soldiers, not the farmers, that drove the mules up and down the mountainsides. The spines of the pack animals sagged incurably under the weight of their contraband loads; the shoulders of the men were rubbed raw and branded by the straps of heavy backpacks.

The poppy harvest had produced new kingdoms with armies that clashed along the shifting borders, the victors exacting gate fees, ferry fees, levies, taxes, protection money, and assorted other penalties.

In the cities to the south and east, the armies bartered the opium harvests for arms to fight wars without beginning or end. In the bleached, burned-out valleys that were eating through the jungle, new man-made sounds filled the air: the chatter of automatic weapons, the belch of grenades, the sudden whine of a bullet.

In the fields to the west, women nicked the plump poppy bulbs and bled them of their precious "tears," catching the sap in tin cans that hung from their necks, while the children rattled dried poppy pods and drew stick figures with twigs in the burnt ocher-colored earth.

Miles away, in his village, Shan heard the woodpecker

tappings of the men who were clearing the land for new opium fields. He heard the pained protest of the trees as they splintered and crashed to the ground. There they would remain until the air had fanned and sucked them tinder dry.

On the day of the burn-off, the young men of the villages would gather at dusk, flaming torches in hand, and swoop down in a pack, hooting and cheering and trailing eddies of fire that whipped through the trees. A child's brigade was stationed at the edge of the clearing. Their job was to heap brush onto the flames.

After the burn-off, while the earth was left to moisten under the ashes, Shan went with the men in search of new fields. Once, down at the Catholic mission school where he was sent to learn his ABCs, one of the nuns saw him break off a piece of dirt and put it in his mouth. "Oh, beast!" she cried, leaving angry finger stripes across his back. "Oh, filthy, dirty!"

But this was a necessary skill: to chew on small clumps of earth; to taste the soil for the sweetness of alkaline, where poppy would grow.

He learned to scoop up the red mud from the riverbeds and roll it into pellets that hardened in the sun and shattered in the breasts of birds. He learned to trap shrews in waters poisoned with aconite root; to shoot the crossbow from a squatting position; to pluck an arrow from behind his ear, and to lick the arrow before sending it into the heart of a tree squirrel.

He memorized the mating songs of birds, the names of wild roots and trees, the laughter of gibbons drunk on berries.

In the clear, cold nights when the village was asleep, he played his flute in a moss-covered hollow, under the stars and the dark goblin faces of the mountain peaks. When he stopped to listen he could hear his tunes—the same wavering tunes sung by the village women while gathering the poppy's tears—being played back to him from the starry reaches of the sky.

His village had an uncommon visitor once: a hunter, white-skinned and hairy as an ape. The hunter was tracking the takin and spoke tenderly of the rare beast as though it were a son. The villagers sat and stared: The white man's face had been fried by the sun; hair grew out of his nose and ears; his smell was beefy; he had the genitals of a horse.

Shan, who had some English by then, was asked to interpret. *Ask him this, ask him that*.

"Ask him," said an old woman, a prankish great-grandmother, "if his turds are white."

Shan hesitated. White turds?

"Go on, ask," said the woman. "Who knows? White people are different. They rot before they die."

"How so?" said Shan.

"Their farts are deadly. A hog would gag."

Shan went up to the hunter. "Do you make white shit?"

The hunter shook with amusement. This was good enough for the old woman. She cackled as if in pain, till her eyes and nose ran and she wet the ground, lifting her skirt and squatting just in time.

Sometime later, when Father returned to the village from one of his campaigns, she told her joke with renewed hilarity, giving Shan a push while she went on about how she had made a monkey out of him.

Father gave a short laugh. "He's dumb, all right," he said of his son. "Twelve years old and still a shrimphead. Show him your thumb, he'll mistake it for your nose. Give him a smooth stone, he'll eat it. He doesn't know a nostril from an asshole. Only he would think white men shit white turds."

Shan, a dreamer rather than a fighter, was the hair that tickled Father's nose. Father didn't suffer deficiencies.

When he noticed that his own son had begun to stutter, he reckoned the only cure would be to knock it out of the boy.

So without warning he struck him across the face—so suddenly and so hard that Shan was spun off his feet and sent staggering. He thought his head had fallen off, until he heard, along the side of his face, a clamor left by the blow.

Father kept up the surprise attacks for days. They came always at least expected moments. In his presence, Shan developed a crouch, ready to dodge the blow. But he was never prepared. Each time the shock was as startling as the first. Each time stars went shooting around his head, his ears rang, and the sting of Father's palm crept like an army of fire ants over the side of his face.

He outgrew the stutter—much later, and not through Father's efforts. He was cured the day he found his mother racked by great angry, ugly sobs—and then heard her curse the world in that unforgettable scream.

Father was right: It took a shock to knock the stutter out of him.

At the mission where he had spent a year in the care of the nuns, there was a servant girl called Nankee who bathed him on Sundays, an hour before mass. She undressed him with the same teasing chant:

Shame, shame,
Puppy, shame,
All the donkeys know your name.

She was an orphan adopted by the nuns, a half-caste with skin the color of coal and eyes the shade of dirty river water. There was something of the wolf in her face: a restless animal look and the hint of a dangerous snout.

It galled her that the nuns made such a fuss over a little outcast like him. All that talk about how clever he was—just because he had learned to read and write before he turned five; just because he could recite the alphabet in English like a parrot, singing the middle section with a slurred *elemen-opee*. They fawned over him as over a monkey with tricks.

In front of the nuns she gave him her strange sinking smile, calling out endearments in a lilting voice. Alone, she bullied him with a pinch here, a wrench there. She would knock his forehead with her sharp elbow, push him off the steps, spill hot soup on him, trip him with her foot—and pretend it was an accident.

But those Sunday baths were the worst. She would scrub him with vigorous spite, muttering, "This is to wash off your sins, little worm . . . this is to cleanse you of your mother's slime . . . " while pouring basin after basin of ice-cold water over his head.

One morning, as she bent over to scratch and scour his head, he turned rabid and sank his teeth into her breast. The girl opened her mouth to scream, but managed only a gasp and a whistle of pain. The basin clattered to the floor. She ran out of the kitchen cupping her breast.

The nuns found him shivering in the bath. Red with anger, one of them went for his ears, boxing and pulling on them. She shook him till his teeth rattled, and called him a savage. Still wet and shivering, he was made to kneel naked in a corner, reminded again and again that his father would hear of his bestiality.

But when Father heard, he surprised the nuns by throwing back his head and howling with laughter, unaware that Shan, in anticipation of his punishment, had already stained his pants in fear.

Nankee never bathed him after that.

Years later, when Father had returned to the south and I was about four, Nankee was trotted out of the mission and into the train that would bring her and Shan, now fourteen years old, to their new home in the lowland capital. She wasn't unhappy about the change. At twenty-five, she was more than ready to find out what the world beyond the mission had to offer, even if it meant a demotion of sorts. At the convent, she had enjoyed seniority as a domestic; in her new home, she would start as washmaid. But in life, a person had to take chances or remain, like a chicken, "happy where your shit falls," as the saying went.

At Father's instructions, they were put on a carriage at the northern terminus, twenty miles south of their village.

He had sent one of his lackeys, a fat, betel-chewing fellow with six fingers on one hand, to fetch the boy and the servant. They stood on the platform while coolies threw coal at the engines and the cars coupled, shunted, and uncoupled. Through the long descent to the south, earth and sky flew past the open window of the carriage. Green and yellow paddy fields swept by; then tea-leaf terraces; then water buffalo, with tiny birds perched on their backs.

The train whistled through narrow black gorges, shooting down toward foothills that had the look of crumpled brown paper. To lean out of the window and see the tail end of the train zigzagging its way down an incline gave one a pain in the pit of the stomach.

At a station in the heart of the dry zone, an army of saffron-robed monks got on board. They were rowdy, arrogant, hard-faced men, swaggering down the aisles and swearing at the timid train conductor for overbooking. They slept in the narrow corridors outside the compartments, strewn about like a shipment of spice-stained sacks.

The next morning, about thirty miles outside the city, Shan was squeezing his way down the crowded corridor when he was caught in a tumult of squabbling monks. They were shouting, cursing, pushing, and kicking at one another like undisciplined schoolboys.

Shan took refuge against an open window, where he was

in danger of falling out or being crushed to death. When Nankee went to look for him, she too was badly frightened: tweaked on the nipples and pinched on the thigh by hands that should have been pressed together in prayer, or clasped around begging bowls.

The monks got off finally at the next-to-last station, leaving the passengers dazed and the train conductor fanning himself with relief.

I had never been on a train when Shan first told me this story, and so I memorized this chronicle of their trip down south. Yet of the day my brother and I first met I have no memory at all.

("Of course you wouldn't remember," he would say. "You were only four. But I remember. You were standing on the steps when we came from the station in the jeep— such a dark little skinny little thing in a blue pinafore. Someone said, 'That's your brother. Give him a kiss.' But you just kissed your hand on the palm and gave it to me.")

Coming south was Nankee's greatest mistake: She felt it from the start and told the other servants so. What a fool she was to leave those good nuns who had treated her like a daughter! And for this: to spend her days beating wet clothes against a washstone and getting headaches from this hellish southern sun. She blamed it all on Shan.

I found her locked in the narrow little broom closet near the kitchen one day, hoarse, sore-fisted from pounding on the door, and beside herself.

"He slapped me and locked me in this hole. Oh, God, I was this far from suffocating!" She grabbed my hand, held it to her chest ("Feel my heart. I almost stopped breathing!") and to her cheeks ("Feel where he slapped me! Lord, now I understand the expression 'I'll slug your face hard enough to break your leg'").

When Father got home I couldn't wait to report the injustice.

"Shan slapped Nankee and shut her in the broom closet. Now she's sick," I said.

Father bit his tongue. "Go find your brother and bring him to me."

When Shan appeared, Father wasted no time. He seized him by the front of his shirt and struck him with his open hand across the face. "Don't you ever hit women," he said, before walking away, his tongue still between his teeth.

It all happened so quickly that it might not have happened at all. But I saw the look on Shan's face as Father pulled it up to his: a cross-eyed look of pure terror; I heard the terrific smack of flesh striking flesh; and now I was left with the casualty I had caused: my brother, still standing where Father had struck him, clenching his fists and fighting back the tears.

I watched in a daze of incomprehension.

Shan was eighteen then—long since a man in my eyes. Weren't grown men supposed to defend themselves from attack? Right or wrong, as a man or as a boy, Father himself would never have taken such abuse. Of that I was certain. And yet his son could take it. Why?

I knew the answer, of course. I could have cried out for having forgotten it: It was simply that we were helpless, we would always be helpless against Father's crushing rule. How could I have thought even for a moment that we stood a chance?

Sick from the weight of my betrayal, I pressed myself to Shan's side. "Please, please forgive me. I'll never tell on you again."

"It's okay," he said, when he had gained control of himself. Then, catching my neck in the crook of his elbow (a sign that we were friends again), he said, "Just don't stick your nose into things you don't understand."

When I was old enough to be curious about such things, when Nankee had eloped with the gardener's cousin and we were recalling the broom closet incident, Shan told me about how she had tried to seduce him.

For weeks she had been giving him signs: letting her blouse fall open to reveal her longish breasts, and casually scratching them; rubbing her crotch, her backside, when she thought he was watching. Full of sly looks and provocations, she followed him around like a puppy eager for a romp or a bone.

Then, one night when the kitchen was dark, she led him to the broom closet on the pretext of showing him a giant bat, but the minute she stepped inside she seized his hand and held it to her scratchy crotch, even working his fingers so they parted the thick scrub to feel the slippery divide.

The expectation of the bat, the sudden sensation of having touched a dead animal, made him shut the door in fright and run.

"Not that I was a virgin, mind you," he said. "Look, I had women even before I came south."

"What? At fourteen? Don't tell lies."

"Would I lie to you? It happened."

"The devil take you and thunder strike you down!"

"The devil and thunder . . . " he said, taking the oath in shorthand, the better to get on with his story:

It was back in his village, on the night of the ceremony marking the boys' coming-of-age. After the ritual slaughter, when the boys had clubbed the screaming cow to death and the carcass had been roasted over an open pit, they sat around the fire and tore off handfuls of stringy meat and washed it down with canteens of toddy.

Then it was time for the chase. They saw the virgin bounding across the field, a swift shadow in the moonlight, and let her gain a head start—to prolong and savor the pursuit. When the girl had covered the proper distance, the boys, drunk on beer and the taste of manhood, ran after her with yelps and hollers taken up by the village dogs.

Shan, who was still two years away from his coming-of-age, was asleep in his hut, untroubled by any inkling of the prank to be played.

In the middle of the night, the door flew open. A body fell on the ground next to him. The door was pulled shut again.

Startled out of sleep, he shrank from the intruder, who was panting heavily and reeking with sweat.

"Virgin meets virgin," a voice on the outside whispered through the thatch.

Inside, Shan made out for the first time the outline of a girl's body. Confused, he started toward the door. The movement sent her whimpering like a little dog.

Outside, the giggles were getting louder.

"Keep the door shut. They might be shy."

"Yes, let them grope in the dark. Let them miss their aim: the wrong parts in the wrong places."

"Even in the dark, he'll rip her apart. . . ."

"Even in the dark, she'll sink her teeth into . . . "

Shan crept toward the door again. The girl started to scream. Outside, the dogs were yowling in harmony. Wanting to silence the girl, he lunged at her, and felt the fabric of her skirt in his hand. The girl pulled away, whinnying, and paid out the long strip of cloth wrapped around her body.

"Listen to her love song."

"A she-leopard in heat."

"She'll show him her colors, like a blue-assed baboon."

"And he'll kiss it in the dark, thinking it's her face."

"You can talk? You with the face of a jackal's ass?"

"Only you would know. You who go sniffing around them."

"Listen, listen . . . "

Shan pulled at the uncoiling fabric. She let go of the cloth and went for his hair, tugging at the roots with menacing growls. He clapped a hand over her mouth; she snapped at the flesh between his thumb and forefinger.

He pushed her down to subdue her, and pinned her to the ground with the weight of his body.

Then he noticed something strange. She wasn't so much struggling as bucking, moving her hips as in a dance. And she wasn't so much growling as letting out a hoarse little song of sighs. Her fingers still scratched at his back, but her legs were wrapped around his waist. Suddenly, silver anklets jangling, she was riding him like a horseman for all she was worth.

He came from a world too remote for belief. But even when I grew older and harder to convince, I was hungry for his recollections of that other life.

"Once, in the jungle, I was alone at night," he would begin—and I was captivated.

In the jungle, night would fall suddenly. But his eyes could pick out the black hollows and cradles of the valleys below, the trees that had turned into spirits of the night.

He came to a grassy shelf, patted the ground before spreading out his tarpaulin sheet, covered himself with his gunny sack, rolled himself up in the sheet, and was asleep before the stars appeared.

A far-away whistle floated across his sleep. It came in twos, first from a great distance like the echo of a flute, then closer and clearer until he knew he was awake, and listening to the song of a golden pheasant.

It was still dark; his skin was cold and damp under the blanket of cloud that hung over those high peaks. But the trees began to fill with the first stirrings of life: a rustling and scratching in the branches, the muted screech of a squirrel, the whoops of the first gibbons in the valleys below.

He listened expectantly for the pheasant's call; the last one still hung in the air. Minutes passed. He heard other bird songs, the mewling of the azure fairybird, the piercing tonk-tonk of the barbet, and wondered if he had only dreamed the pheasant.

He rose, rolled up the gunny sack in his sheet, stuffed the bedding in his monkey-skin bag, and started through the dense foliage. Beneath his feet, without warning, the heavy shroud of mulch gave way. He plummeted down through space, grazing aerial roots and giant tree ferns, his fall at last broken by a brambled outcropping. The monkey-skin bag was caught on the branch of a dead ironwood tree.

Through the green-black clusters of lace, woven where the towering trees met together high above, the first quiet light of day filtered through in shafts. Beneath him the valley stretched out to touch the feet of the distant snow mountains.

The furrowed ridges changed from gray to rose as the sky turned red behind the mountains. A bird flew overhead, soaring toward the sun in a harlequin blaze. Just before it disappeared, he recognized the tail of a golden pheasant.

He had seen it: that rarest of birds, soaring east early one morning, the sun on its wings!

At other times, he would begin his stories with: "When I go back to the mountains . . . " As a child I came to dread the threat in that phrase and needed to ask each time, "Will I go with you?"

"You think I'd go without you?" he'd say. "I'll take you to the secret caves. I'll teach you to hunt. We'll pack our bags with sticky rice and saltfish and climb high into the snow mountains to look for the coffin tree."

I was too young and troublesome to be included in his to-ings and fro-ings, but from time to time he would let me in on a new discovery: a warehouse piled to the rafters with rice bags, where we played hide-and-seek; a rusty green tank the size of a public pool where we felt the moss with the tips of our toes and swam with the bullfrogs and minnows; the depot of derelict army trucks that served as covered wagons in our games of cowboys-and-Indians.

He taught me to swim, climb trees, build a fire, and shoot a catapult. He taught me to roll birdshot pellets out of river mud, to scale fish freshly caught from the lake, and to eat watermelon rind. These were arcane and forbidden skills, learned on the sly.

Without him, the world might have remained only as large as the compound in which I lived: a house bordered by hedges clipped in the shape of regimental birds just high enough to conceal the concertina coils of barbed wire.

Without him, I would never have dared creep through the holes in the hedges under the watchman's nose—let alone cross the lake in that makeshift raft, or find my way to quarters as insalubrious as the Thieves' Market.

It was in this section of town straddling the Chinese and Indian quarters that he gambled away his allowance week after week. And it was here that his satellites lived: Billy Wing Ong, the "poker king"; Ajax, the ex-convict; and Danson da Silva, the asthmatic sissy. It was no accident that his friends were all inferiors, poorer or weaker than he. He sought and bought loyalty among the downtrodden. In return for his favors, he got a slavish devotion not easily exacted among equals, and that gratitude was sufficient reward.

At home, his drifter's ethic provoked deep sighs and head shaking. "He'll end up in the sewer, what a disgrace!" My aunts were as disturbed by the disgrace as by the sewer. "What a rotten egg he turned out to be, after all we've done for him!" They spoke from their hearts, having advanced him money time and again without hope of recovery.

And the worst of it was that they loved him so, the waster!

It wasn't simply the way he swept the women off their feet, literally, in sudden outbursts of exuberance and good-will—or squeezed the breath out of them in bear hugs that could only be explained by the old folk idiom of a "tickle in the heart." It was a feeling he left that though he took without compunction he would give even more in return; and it was a measure of his charm that those from whom he took didn't hold it against him that he seldom had anything to give.

With Father's generous allowance and reserves from our aunts' savings, he bailed Billy out of actionable gambling debts—of which he himself had more than his share. To Ajax he gave the shirt off his back. (Ajax's chronic unemployment wasn't due solely to his criminal record. Despite his brutish physique, he was as lazy as a lap dog, letting his fingernails grow into talons and his nose sprout blackheads the size of potato eyes.)

Danson was a charity case of a different sort. Shan offered him protection from a society that took umbrage and turned mean at the sight of a man with a mincing gait, a prissy umbrella, and a precise middle part down a pompadour. Fearing random reprisals from the man in the street, Danson paid the price of protection by suffering other abuses at the hands of his protectors.

In Shan's room, he consented on idle afternoons to play the whipping boy, while Shan, Billy, and Ajax took turns holding a knife to his neck, or threatening to bring down the cherished umbrella on his symmetrically parted head.

I saw this myself one day. Riding my bicycle round and round the house, I heard a strangled voice and hoisted myself up onto the high windowsill, where I could watch their game unseen.

"No, no; Danson begs you!" In a woman's frightened falsetto, he had turned himself, the supplicant, into the third person—disassociating himself from the voice of abject cowardice that escaped his endangered throat.

"Say it again," demanded the bully-boy chorus.

"Danson begs you."

"Again."

"I've said Danson begs you!" (petulance in his voice now).

"Nicely."

"Dan-son-begs-yooooo!"

When the door opened an hour later, they emerged once more as a group, shining with solidarity. Danson had composed himself, umbrella in hand, a smile on his face, glad to be one of the boys—gladder still, no doubt, to be alive.

Bristling at the company Shan kept, my aunts discouraged his shadows from showing up at the house too often, and so he took to passing the time on their territory, in the Thieves' Market area. There, Billy's mother sold snuff bottles that were cheap imitations of tourmaline and coral, jade and hornbill, amber and moss agate. There, Ajax sponged off his sister's family, who ran a furniture store. There, Danson taught kindergarten in the parochial school behind the restaurant famous for its steamed crab claws. And there, the old coffin tree merchant read fortunes, palms, and tea leaves.

The soothsayer was another of Shan's discoveries. Here was a man dwarfed by circumstance but still larger than life. He was old, he was sick; he had lost all his money. But his powers! Shan spoke of them in hyperbole—not of speech, but of facial expression. (In trying to convey the improbable or the unbelievable, my brother tried persuasion by mime rather than speech.)

"Imagine a man," he would say to me, "who knows everything."

"What do you mean *everything*?"

My skepticism made him turn to mime. "He knows

divination . . . " (eyes widening to take in the future); "he knows sorcery . . . "(fingers twitching and arms waving with a magician's flourishes); "he can go into a trance" (eyes squeezed shut, hands outstretched and groping) "and see what's coming."

At seventeen, I was beginning to find these theatrics embarrassing. Sensing this, he said, "You don't believe me. I'll just have to take you to see for yourself. But you say one word to anyone and I'll . . . you just better not say anything or I'll catch hell."

It was a section of town I had never seen. After innumerable side streets, where bandicoots and mangy dogs snuffled in the stinking drains, we crossed a low macadamized bridge over a foul canal. Peeling mint-green and fuchsia sampans plied the muddy water. Where the bridge ended, the first row of shops began. Bright sails of fabric billowed out into the street from the narrow doorways and almost hid the seamstresses who sat behind sewing machines that looked and yapped like small black dogs.

We squeezed through the crowded pathways between the army-navy surplus stores, where jungle boots and fatigues lay in disordered heaps among sextants, brass lanterns, compasses, coiled lines, weather-beaten hatches, and teakwood chests filled with small boxes within boxes.

We saw intent-looking foreigners scavenging through shops crammed with carved cabinets, roll-top desks, brass beds inlaid with mother-of-pearl, copper candelabra and wicker bird cages, teakwood plantation chairs, old doors and benches, wrought-iron flower stands, money boxes, coal irons, glass globes, brass spittoons, ceramic vats and urns, copper drums, lacquer cupboards, and three-sided wedding beds.

We passed rows of acrid spice shops with their displays of jute-lined baskets overflowing with red and green chillies, yellow turmeric, white rice, purple brinjals, earth-colored cumin and coriander, and mud-covered "thousand-year-old eggs." We passed rows of apothecary stores hung with desiccated cobra bladders and pig intestines, and lined with jars of dried mushrooms and sea horses, powdered roots and rhino horn.

Leaving behind the last of the shops, we followed back alleys too narrow even for bicycles and rickshaws, where centuries' worth of refuse and filth seemed to have settled into maggoty compost heaps along the walls. At the end of a gray-green façade that bore the faded letterings of a warehouse, Shan stopped and motioned me through a small opening in the wall.

"He's probably asleep," he said; and for a moment I could not believe that we had arrived at our destination, that here in the seamiest side of the city I had ever seen, with its rotting stench and the slime underfoot, was the fortune-teller's abode. I had expected a better address.

I hesitated at the threshold. All I could see was a dark cubicle. The door—the expanding metal kind—was open a crack, but Shan had to push heavily with his shoulder to pry it apart. Once inside, I saw a small square table and a wooden stool, and, above, a makeshift altar holding a ceramic image of an obese, placid god. Its naked and distended belly had been draped with strands of jasmine blossoms long past their prime. The air was stale, overripe, and unpleasantly sweet.

Shan lit the kerosene lamp that stood on the rusty table, and I saw a human shape among the sudden shadows that leapt across the walls. It was behind me, lying on its side on a low platform bed, curled like a fetus and absolutely still.

Shan leaned over the bed and spoke into its face. "Grandpa? Are you well? I brought my sister."

I looked down at a creature that reminded me of something I had seen in an illustration rather than in the flesh: a fairy-tale picture of those mischievous, troubling little beings with huge heads and spindly bodies that came out of hiding if you ever got lost in the woods.

A pair of outsized, bulging eyes looked up at me. "Come, girl," said the wizened figure. "Give your hand." The voice had a hollow resonance, as if it rose out of a deep well. I obeyed by sitting at the edge of his bed, mindful of his brittle-looking knees, and held out my hand. He took it in his fingers, which were so small and shriveled they could have been pickled. In his other hand he was playing with a small pellet of some soft dark substance.

He felt my palm as a blind man might, staring into space with a stunned look. I took in the sordid neglect everywhere apparent in that cell. Above the bed, torn faded scrolls with indecipherable symbols and characters papered the wall. In the flickering light I could see, along the corners of the walls, what looked like stalagmites of grease.

Shan had moved to the other end of the room, where he was seated at the table on which lay a pile of old *Life* magazines. "So, Grandpa?" he said suddenly, breaking into the cheerful singsong that the healthy affect in the presence of the sick. "How goes it? Anything new? What can I bring you? Noodles? Dumplings? Sugarcane juice?"

But the old man was intent on the topography of my palm. Rubbing his fingers across it, he continued to stare agog into the distance with that same look of wonder over a startling private vision. "All those stars!" he said, fingering the crisscrossing lines in my palm. "So many stars in one hand. They fell from heaven and you caught them. That kind of strength means courage, great courage."

I laughed and looked at Shan. He was frowning at me, while his head was seized by a tremor of disapproval and warning against any irreverence I might show.

The old man, still looking past me, said, "You laugh? Courage is something, girl. It sees you through times. Riches come, riches go. I was rich once; who would think that now? Now I'm just a dreamer, nothing more. It's this stuff." He held out the little black pellet he had been rolling between thumb and forefinger. "It makes you dream like anything."

Shifting my foot uneasily, I kicked something under the bed and bent down to look. It was a tray holding an odd-shaped pipe and what looked like an assortment of surgical instruments. From under the bed, I caught a whiff of something strong and insufferably sweet. It hit me like a slap in the face, like a reprimand for my unhealthy curiosity.

I looked up at Shan to signal my desire to leave, but the old man was telling, or rather chanting, a story in his hollow, echoey voice: "Yes, rich I was. A timber merchant I was. Up in the north I traded. Selling planks was my business. Coffin planks. My coolies I took and walked and walked, through the rain forests, searching for coffin trees. Not easy to find, girl. With donkeys we went, up and down those frightful slopes, slipping and sliding, till we saw one. Then we cut it down. Then we sawed it, *chaw-chaw-chaw*. The planks! They were a hundred pounds each. No laughing matter. Then back we went to the border town. My money I made on guess how many trees? My money I made on twenty trees. Twenty trees, that's all. No more."

He had let go of my hand now and had turned to lie on his back, his hands clasped behind his neck, striking a grotesquely insouciant pose. "Once," he said, more conversationally now, "I saw the biggest one of them all. What a tree! It alone would have made my fortune. It was . . . ah, don't try to imagine. It went up into the sky, up and up, higher than two hundred feet, I swear. And I, yes this broken-down addict, I was the one who found it.

"I found it up there . . . on the high ridges of the Great Snow Range, where the snow lies thick on everything. It stood at the fork of a river stream, all alone. I never saw anything like it. The bark was different. The color was different. But it was a coffin tree, no mistake. It grew higher than two hundred feet. Believe it.

"The snow was melting here and there. But the dwarf bushes still had frost on them. I'll wait till spring, I said to myself. I'll wait till I can see the cherry bushes once more.

"For nothing I waited. Useless. I went back to the mountains in the spring. The tree was gone. Gone. Who knows where?"

When we were back out on the street, making our way home, I said, "Some fortune-teller. His head has gone soft. Why didn't you tell me he was an opium addict?"

Shan said, "Opium addict, booze addict, what's the difference? I wanted you to hear what he had to say. You're lucky he even talked to you."

I said, "I don't understand what he had to say. What was all that about the coffin tree?"

"You know what's your trouble?" Shan said. "Your trouble is you're just a young thing." He knew how to get even with me. "I thought you were old enough to understand. Someday we're going to find that tree."

I said, "Shan. Don't be a dreamer."

"We're going," he said with maddening conviction—the conviction of a creed I would discover only years later.

"Not me," I said. "What for? Shan, when are you going to start paying Auntie back? You should be earning money, not messing around with opium eaters."

"Just a young thing," he said. "I should have known better."

9

In the early days at 3 East, Paddy and I, both unable to sleep, had stayed up through the night shift together, slouching over the Scrabble board until the words reversed themselves and the letters somersaulted before my aching eyes. Others were struggling with sleep, too—Brian and Helga, usually; and Robin and Jolene, who woke up too early.

But we were the only two who remained awake from the 10:00 P.M. medication to the nurse's rounds at three, and at times till seven in the morning, when the night staff signed off with the written report.

By my second month, Paddy had stopped talking completely. Yet even before that, it was through his letters that he chose to speak to me:

If you think about it you'll see what a good idea it is for people to write letters when they already live in the same ward. The letter method is convenient and practical for people like us who are fairly tied up with activities during the day, yet the knowledge of physical closeness precludes the feeling of obligation. This is just a thought—not a missing link of transcendence or communication, as I was inclined to believe when the idea first occurred to me. You do not owe me a response. And don't feel pressure simply out of spite because I said not to feel any pressure.

P

I'd find his notes usually on my breakfast tray, tucked into the folds of the napkin.

Last night, awake, I said to myself, "How peculiar the clock sounds, ticking the way it is!" And I remembered an experiment I heard about once, where a man was put in a shaft that went down into the earth, and the shaft was closed so that he would be alone for twelve hours or so. The man said later that he could concentrate, as time went on, on listening to the beating of his own heart. Did he say to himself, I wondered, "God! This silence is great!"?

I think about words and silences because of an argument my brother and I had when I was 10. He was 17 then and he had just told me a story about a Zen Buddhist who, with a friend, was watching a sunset in silence. After a time the friend said, "What a beautiful sunset!" To which the Buddhist replied, "Yes, but what a shame to say so."

I said then that the Buddhist was absolutely right and that his friend had ruined everything. My brother said no, that the Buddhist had been wrong in correcting his friend, because he was in effect saying, "How sensitive am I and how un-(sic) are you."

I don't want to kill or degrade the mystery of things, yet I don't want to maintain an agnostic superior silence. But it seems I go to either extreme at different times.

About the difficult things: Maybe I think, If you can say it, it can go away. Like the childhood guilt game where someone tells you, "Every time you say you don't

believe in fairies, somewhere a little fairy dies." So I and
the girl I used to play with would say it over and over
again, so that eventuallly we would have killed so many
that it would no longer matter.

Comrade, I am such an uneven mental split, like an
earthquake tremor shifted half my brain down a few centi-
meters.

Once, after the game of charades with Robin, he handed
me this note:

I chose Tristan and Isolde not because of the romance, but
because the language of the story was so strange. It was
like reading a book that was written by a parrot, or some
such animal.

Our long nights of Scrabble came to an end when the
increase in his dosage of Thorazine knocked him out by
midnight. Alone with my insomnia, I counted the hours in
bed, in the room I shared with Sarah and Helga. Sarah lay
in the shadows cast by her potted plants that hung across the
window. She slept deeply, her long dark hair spread out on
the pillow, her arms around a stuffed raccoon, while the
numbers on the digital clock beside her bed fell off with
small clicks minute by minute. On the other side of the
room, Helga lay flat on her back as though tied down at the
arms and legs by invisible strings, muddling through sleep
with gurgles and moans, and reaching out now and then to
feel her wig of flat golden curls that lay on the bedside table.

In the daylight hours, Paddy wove in and out of our
group routines, less and less within reach. He still played his
guitar, but the chords were loud and dissonant. Once I saw
him stroke the instrument like a live pet, feeding it a cookie
which he slid, gingerly, underneath the strings into the
hollow of the guitar. I saw him drink the water from jars

containing plant cuttings. I saw him trying to eat off his tray through the vertical slats in the tray trolley, laboriously picking out kernels of corn and peas. I saw him place an orange on the sink of each bathroom, then tie a red ribbon around a water faucet.

I reread his letters, wondering how it was possible he could have written them just weeks ago.

Here is a vignette from my past: Once I was involved in a lawn-mower project. I'd learned quite a lot, testing those handle grips. One morning I hadn't gone to bed till 5 A.M. I woke up around 10 or 11 and was walking back from the mailbox. Ten minutes previously I had been asleep. A shy and suspicious fellow from Nashville appeared at the other end of the sidewalk and fairly shouted: "Are you gonna get them 3 lawnmowers fixed today . . . OR NOT?"

At that hour, still absorbed in the remaining fragments of dreams, letting the day in slowly, the shock of his nasal harshness was like ramming sandspurs down my ears with Q-tips, and I let out an anguished scream.

I had a dream about your father as being a bald, Oriental, sadistic type, wearing a long robe with stars and half-moons printed on it. He was interrogating political prisoners by tying them to a cross on the floor and flogging their chests with a leather strap. I knew he was your father because there was an accompanying monologue that said so.

I believe I can starve hundreds of people by going on a twelve-day fast myself with no water for the last day and a half. Then, when I got really emaciated, I could go out onto the grass and twist myself into an arduous yoga position, remaining still for two hours at a time. Then others who witnessed the sanctity of my suffering would be obligated to take at least as much upon themselves.

A possible way out from my overwhelming rage: I have been imagining there is a piece of iron somewhere inside me from which I can draw strength. This way, when I feel the shovels piercing my throat and going deeper, I also sometimes sense a satisfying dull sound of the shovel blade striking against the iron which is my core. This sound says that for the moment, the intruder has gone as far as he can go, yet I am still alive and well.

Augustine said, "So a man becomes more and more shrouded in darkness so long as he pursues willingly what he finds in his weakness is more easy to receive."

Please do not think that I am trying to help you with this package of medieval (midevil?) piety.

I get hooked into infinity trying to explain, all the while instructing you and other victims not to think of a giraffe.

He was crawling about the rooms by now, gamey in the flowered tunic which he'd worn for days. His face was ravaged to the point of sweetness; his smile was slack and foamy. His hollow, dark-ringed eyes seemed to melt into themselves.

Robin snatched away a piece of steel wool just as he was about to put it in his mouth. At the nurse's station, she stood and cried. "Do something, please! He's suffering!"

"We have. He's on different medication now. It will take a while."

"But he hasn't slept in *four days*. How can he go on like this?" Overwrought, she was rubbing her scarred wrists.

Paddy emerged out of a shower stall, fully clothed but soaked through. He staggered down the hall like a drunk in a rainstorm and crashed into the doctor's scales that stood against the wall. Clinging to the vertical shaft, he sat down on the scales, making noises that sounded like "Oh, wow!"

Winston came to pull him up and lead him to the room they shared.

Later, after Winston had helped him get out of his wet clothes, I went to look in on him. He was sprawled across his bed on his stomach, shirtless, but in dry jeans. The floor was littered with the pillows and sheets he had stripped off the bed. He opened his eyes as I approached the bed.

"Can't you sleep?" I asked.

He shook his head.

I went around to the other side of his bed and sat at the edge. His hair was still wet and fell across the side of his face. He looked like every trite version of the suffering Christ.

I ran my fingers very lightly, scarcely touching his skin, up and down his back—until his breathing had settled into a steady, restful snore.

He slept through the afternoon and the night. The next morning he took his place at the breakfast table for the first time in days.

Letty arrived on the ward late one night, slumped in a wheelchair and trailing bottles and tubes. But by the next morning she was full of fight. Wrapped in a frayed seersucker bathrobe, she had shed the IV and wheeled herself into the dining room without help.

"Nothing like making an entrance," she said, as we looked up from the table. She addressed us out of the side of her mouth. There were bruises under her eyes that gave her a fierce, pugilistic look. She had picked herself up from a terrific brawl and was ready to go another round, black eyes notwithstanding.

"I like the rules here, I really like them," she said. "You come in half dead and they refuse to bring you breakfast. Get it yourself, they tell you. But nicely, with a smile. They all smile like Moonies here, have you noticed? The same damned smile that makes you want to ask, Which twin has the lobotomy? They make us get our own breakfasts because we're not supposed to be *physical* invalids, see?"

She raised a thin, veiny hand to an eyebrow. "God, my head!" Then she closed her eyes, observing a moment of silence worthy of the dead. But the next minute she was renewed, casting about the room and spoiling for a fight.

"What are all you young girls doing here?" Her eyes settled on Robin. "Wait till you're my age. Once you're fifty it's over, sweetheart. It's downhill from thirty, but fifty? Fifty's the end. Your kids are gone, your husband has no stomach for you. With all the face lifts and ass lifts in the world —do you know there's a doctor in Brazil who actually does operations to lift your sagging ass? Expensive. But for the woman who has everything? No, with all the help in the world, you can't fight turning fifty."

When the staff trooped in with their trolley of manila folders for the morning report, she clucked in annoyance at the interruption, then shook her head in disbelief as the reports were read out loud:

"Night shift reported a quiet evening. Patient committee met to discuss Brian's farewell party. Sarah was elected emcee. She seemed comfortable in the role of leader and organizer, but became withdrawn by the end of the evening. Jolene complained of dizziness and went to bed shortly after medication. Brian expressed the need to talk about his anxiety over leaving. Afterwards, he appeared more relaxed and took a walk with Paddy and Winston. Paddy indicated discomfort on the tongue and throat due to medication. Helga seemed upset at the prospect of her CT brain-scan tomorrow and expressed the fear that it would damage her brain waves and change her aura. Maria continues to worry about her father's illness and hopes to get permission to visit him at the next pass-and-privilege meeting. The new patient, Letty, came in at midnight from Intensive Care, where she had spent four days recovering from a suicide attempt by drug overdose. She still seems angry at having failed."

"My, my, my," Letty broke in. "I'll be careful not to have an affair in this place."

Helga shifted her chair a little closer to Letty. "Worry

not," she said. "At first it makes the face red to hear such things about yourself. But soon you will be accustomed. In life one can get accustomed to anything. I knew a woman once, a yew-ish writer . . .

"A yewish writer," Helga repeated, abandoning her confidential tone when she realized we were all listening. "She lived next door to me. One day, she moved. Not far, just to the next street. She asked: Can she leave some belongings in my basement? Well, why not? So she brought boxes to my house. That was five years ago. And do you know, she never took them back? Never? 'Tomorrow I'll take them away,' she told me every time. Or next week, or next month. But for five years! Then one day I had enough. I threw everything *aus, aus*.

"But in the meantime, I am accustomed to this strangeness. I just say to myself, *Ja*, what can you expect of a woman who sucks up the roaches—live roaches—in her house with a vacuum cleaner? No, I'm telling the truth. I saw myself this terrible habit."

"Hey, that's some kind of story," said Letty. Then she whistled. "Brother. This is wild stuff. Get me out of here."

A few days later she took me aside, placing her arm around me conspiratorially. "I bet you didn't know what Maria does for a living?"

"I think she told us. She's a secretary."

"Yes, but for whom?"

"For the government?"

Letty laughed. "That's one way of putting it. More precisely for the executive branch. Even more precisely, for the White House. Where in the White House? Are you ready for this? Our timid little Maria with the ECT bruises on her brow answers mail for the President of the United States of America. Now, doesn't that just beat all? All those little old ladies in Podunk who write to the Prez and have their prayers answered when they get a reply on White House stationery . . . if they only knew their letters were getting answered by a full-blown psychotic—I don't mean the President, ha-ha! Heck, she can't even remember last month. The ECT's wiped out a year's worth of memory. Think of that."

One afternoon at Group, Maria was reporting on her visit with her sick father when, her voice trembling, she said, "One of these days I must face the fact of my father's death; and I'm afraid I won't know how. It's true. A woman in her forties can so dread the loss of a father that she goes to bed clutching a handkerchief. The tears come on in my sleep." She began to cry softly. "My father is the only thing about me worth saving. This shell I'm in, this shell you see, holds the dregs of an organism that was all wrong from the start. The world sees a two-headed monster and agrees that it were better dead. But what about the deformities that aren't visible to the naked eye? What about the two-headed monsters that are born within some of us but remain in hiding?

"My point is," Maria said, "my father is dying. It is far worse than my dying. Some people here . . . " she began to falter ". . . think they have the option of ending their lives. I just want to say, life is so precious."

When I looked up, Letty was wiping her eyes. "I know you mean me, Maria," she said at last. "You think it's unfair that your father is trying so hard to live when I've been trying so hard to die. But I've had my share of unfairness, too. Things simply refuse to go right for me. And they begin to pile up. You know how it is. A son, an only son, dies of leukemia at twenty-four. Unable to bear it, you try to kill yourself. Attempt number one. But they get you to the hospital in time. Meanwhile, the husband gets the news. He drives to the hospital like a madman and has a wreck that cripples him for life. So you try to end your life again. Attempt number two. Not right away, of course—but when you see how things are never going to get better, only worse, because there is no repairing what's happened—just as there was no repairing my father's life. He was a sad, disturbed man. He fought a losing battle. I can remember from when I was this small: those long periods when he was off at one mental home after another. In the end he hung himself. In a hospital bed sheet, of all things. They knew he was suicidal, and they thought they'd removed all dangerous objects. But my father! He was a clever man, even when he was down in the dumps."

We listened with our heads bowed. Maria had stopped crying. Letty was calm. "I once asked a doctor," she said after a long silence, "one of the ones that had quote saved my life unquote. I asked him whether it wasn't tyranny to dictate to a person who has chosen to give up the struggle that he must live. He answered me in such a funny tone of voice. Like he was embarrassed or something. He said, 'We feel that when a person has an overwhelming desire to end his life, it is a dis-ease.' Like a discomfort, you know. Was he ever off the mark! It isn't discomfort, or *dis*-ease as he put it. It's this aching, throbbing, god-awful incurable pain— and it's known as life. When will the doctors learn: It isn't death that's the disease."

10

Our fathers! Their ghosts hovered about us in that ward. I was part of that little community of wronged children, but I couldn't bring myself to join the free-for-all by giving my father a public drubbing. So many things stood in the way: propriety, shame, pain, the taboo against bad-mouthing a parent. Also, I wondered how I could recount some of the stories about him without having the group burn him in effigy. His response to madness, for instance. How would it sit with the inmates of 3 East?

I was thinking of the year I turned thirteen, when I got up from bed one morning to open the shutters and found a strange man under my bedroom window. He was sitting cross-legged on the ground, his back to me. He was wearing a latrine cleaner's loincloth but was naked from the waist up. His skin was almost black, and his head was closely shaven.

He had surrounded himself with an assortment of worthless odds and ends: empty soda bottles, an old milk tin, a bundle of twigs, a frayed gunny sack, and a ball of twine.

I went outside. "What are you doing?" I said—a foolish question, since he was clearly doing nothing. It was only then that I saw, by the smile on his face, that he wasn't quite right in the head. Seeing me standing over him, he raised his hand and blessed me like a priest with a sign of the cross. In front of him, lying like a dead porcupine, was a huge jackfruit. He began to pick at its spiky skin, trying to break it open with his bare fingers, which were coated with the sticky sap oozing out of its stalk.

I went round to the servants' kitchen at the back of the house and found the usual cauldron of rice gruel bubbling on the coal stove. I picked up a shallow aluminum bowl— the kind the servants used—and filled it with a heaping ladle of the rice. Curious, the cook followed me outside.

I handed the vagrant the bowl. When he didn't respond, I set it on the ground in front of him, as if feeding an animal. He studied the bowl for a while, then began to search through his things until he pulled out of his gunny sack a cheap bamboo flute—the kind with the mottled stain that the tourists seemed to go for. He lifted the flute to his mouth and began to play, his naked ribs rising and falling as he breathed in and out, while his eyes remained fixed on the bowl of rice.

The cook watched him for a few minutes, arrested by the strange soundless performance: the stops in the flute had been stuffed with some dark, puttylike substance. The cook burst out laughing. "Lunatic!" he said, and went to tell the other servants.

The vagrant stopped playing, set down his flute, and began to scoop up the rice with his fingers: slowly, almost delicately. He ate every grain.

Afterwards, rising on one leg and trying to keep his balance, he shook out his sack and gathered up his things. He swung the bag over his shoulder, paved the ground before him with a sign of the cross, hopped, gave another blessing, and proceeded like this out the gate and into the street. Confronted by traffic, he set the other foot down and walked away.

Later that day I heard voices arguing in the kitchen. The cook was complaining that the largest, ripest jackfruit which he'd had his eye on had disappeared from the tree.

The vagrant was there the next morning, settling down in the same spot beneath my bedroom window. From then on, he came every day (giving me the sign of the cross each time) and left at dusk when the mosquitoes swarmed in from the thick fruit trees. In the stinging, late-summer heat of the afternoons, he would take shelter in the shady orchards, picking through the bruised or rotting fruit that lay on the ground. We had mangoes, mariannes, guavas, plums, sugar apples, custard apples, almonds, and other fruit that ripened and fell faster than we could eat them. Sometimes he sat for hours leaning against the tamarind tree, riffling the blades of sere grass, rearranging his junk, or blowing on his stopped-up flute. I saw him eat a piece of dirt once, chewing carefully, with relish almost, before spitting out the grit.

I took him food from the kitchen—openly at first, then stealthily. I had heard the cook say to one of the washer-women, "So now I'm cooking for the crazies, too! This one is no fool. He'll act like a child and shit on your doorstep. Cunning."

One afternoon, the vagrant sat by the front gate making no move to leave, even though dusk had brought the attack squadron of mosquitoes. The gardener had swept up the cut grass from the edges of the lawn and was about to shut the main gate when he saw the seated figure.

"All right, madman. Out! Disappear!" he ordered.

The vagrant looked up and smiled—shyly, as though he had just received a compliment—and remained sitting.

"I said get out!" the gardener repeated.

The gardener's wife sensed trouble. She was a waddling, flat-footed woman about twice her husband's size in girth and, perhaps for that reason, fond of rushing to his defense with mindless protectiveness. She disappeared and returned in a short time with a long stick, with which she poked at the vagrant—but from the back, cautiously, as if testing a snake that might turn and strike. The man worried at the stick a little, but stayed put.

By this time, my aunts were watching from the kitchen door. Auntie Rosie's face was like a dried plum, dark and puckered. She began to snap her knuckles. "Call the police, call the police," she kept repeating to herself, softly, almost absent-minded in her panic. She had a child's faith in the power of the police. She sometimes even prayed to them.

The gardener was getting purple in the face and was shouting out enraged questions. ("Shall I clobber you, lunatic? Shall I kick your ass?") The wife continued her ineffectual prodding.

"Wait," I said. I went up to the vagrant and gave him my hand. "Come."

He took it without hesitation, got up, and followed me. I led him past the tall wrought-iron gate; past the staid brick houses in our neighborhood that stood almost hidden behind waxy hedges, at the end of long gravel driveways. The winding, mile-long road intersected with a main thoroughfare; and here I disengaged my hand from his and hurried back home, not daring to look back to see if he was following.

"Go wash your hand," said Auntie Lily as soon as I got back. "With Dettol." She was relieved to see me, but too angry to show it.

"What disease the man has you never know," I heard her say to the others. "The child has just become a young lady . . . touching a man is bad enough . . . but a madman!"

Summer was ending. It was still stifling and hot. The

sun was trapped behind the swelling monsoon clouds; the days grew dark and short. When the first mango shower broke through, it landed on parched, fissured ground. The large drops of moisture fell far apart at first, leaving small stains, then coming down smaller and closer to cover the ground with the color of wet earth. I could feel the dampness fill my nostrils with the muddy smell of the monsoons.

One afternoon, I heard the gardener shouting excitedly. I thought at first he had seen a burglar, so urgent were his cries. But he was raging over a corner of the lawn that had been littered with debris. As he stood there, empty bottles and stones were flying in over the hedge and landing on the grass a short distance from him.

I followed him as he rushed outside. We found the vagrant standing by the hedge with a large cardboard box out of which he was drawing the bric-a-brac aimed at our lawn. He went about it almost playfully, but it was clear he intended to complete his task, bottle by bottle, stone by stone.

"Son of a pig!" shouted the gardener, who was a Muslim and cursed accordingly. Then, to himself, "Lunatic!" He was trembling with anger, but afraid to approach the madman. He went back inside the house—to fetch reinforcements, presumably.

As luck decreed, it was at this moment that Father returned home in his limousine. The gardener's shouts had drawn a small crowd of servants from the neighborhood; and seeing that something was amiss as soon as he got out of the car, Father went outside to investigate. The madman apparently had thrown his last bottle. He was resting in the empty cardboard box with an air of accomplishment. But Auntie Lily, whose nerves had loosened her tongue, appeared by Father's side. She knew this would happen, she said. Let a madman have the run of the house and sooner or later he'll behave like one. It was the child that had encouraged him. She knew this would happen.

"What's this? What's this?" Father's voice turned high-pitched and unstable. "You allowed a madman into the house?" Lily, realizing her mistake, began to squeak in alarm. "Not me, not me. This one," she insisted, pointing at me. But Father was oddly oblivious to me and kept yelling at Lily. "You exposed the child to him?" He strode into the house, tongue between the teeth, leaving Lily whimpering and running from the gardener to Rosie to me, crying, "Pray he won't find the gun. No. Quick, hide the gun. He'll shoot, I swear he'll shoot."

It all seemed a lot of playacting to me. The madman was no longer active in any case. But Father emerged a moment later, still in a temper. He stormed outside the gate once more, searching for something.

Among the crowd that had gathered was a boy, a servant's son, who was holding a bucket and a fishing rod. Father went up to him and pulled the rod out of his hand without a word.

All of a sudden I saw what was coming. "Father, please!" I pleaded, with more passion than I'd ever dared display. "He's crazy. He doesn't know what he's doing. He hasn't hurt anyone."

But there was no stopping him. He approached the madman, cracking the thin bamboo rod in front of him like a lion tamer in a circus ring. The gawking servants followed.

As the crowd closed in, the madman showed signs of concern. He was sane enough to perceive that danger was imminent, but had somehow got himself stuck in the cardboard box and was having trouble pulling himself out. At the last moment he toppled over on his side, and this dislodged him at last. But he was too slow.

I had seen enough; I wasn't going to stay for the inevitable savagery. But even before I could make it back into the house, I heard the whistle of the bamboo rod—and then the shrill expression of pain. Then came another whip, another scream, followed by a whip-whip-whip.

After that, I heard only the loud wailing that seemed to go on and on before the madman managed to make his getaway, crying and running down the street.

Later, when I was sitting in the dark of my room, the door opened, letting in the light from the hallway, and I looked up to see my father standing at the door. The light was behind him and concealed his expression, but his voice sounded unusually tentative and awkward as he said, "Well, I got rid of him. But I'm off to the hospital. It isn't much. I caught a fishhook in my thumb."

He stuck out his hand to show me. Against the light I saw the silhouette of his thumb, sprouting the small sharp point of a fishhook.

Just for a moment I wondered if it was possible to bleed to death from a fishhook. No, it was unlikely. But I found no comfort in this—only in thinking that maybe there was some crude justice, after all.

Father was so good at impersonating God that he seemed almost incapable of getting hurt or bleeding. It wasn't just at home, in his private domain, but out in the world at large that people tended to give him right of way. He had no challengers as far as I was concerned.

Dwarfed by his shadow and aware of my own insignificance, I was more servile than the servants. I hastened to obey his orders, to give to his questions only those answers I thought he wished to hear, to regale him with only those stories fit for his amusement. I felt it unseemly to sit still in his presence; I felt I should be moving, doing, achieving in the way that seemed second nature to him.

But seeing me breathless and clumsy with haste, he would wrinkle his brow in exasperation and say, "Here, what's the hurry? Slow down, slow down." Yet when I began to recount a day in school, I detected within minutes a loss of interest: I saw it in his eyes—that abstracted look caused by thoughts unrelated to me—and in his fingers, which began a busy scribbling on the surface of a table or his thigh. I always wondered about those illegible words—were they codes? sentences? the text of speeches he was drafting?—until I found the courage to ask him one day.

He laughed, surprised I had noticed the habit, and said, "It's nothing. When I'm bored I just write words that come into my head. Sometimes just my signature, again and again."

That kind of bluntness was Father's strong suit. It arose out of a perfect disregard for the other person.

There was a time when I read into his remoteness a grudge held against me. I had caused an unforgivable accident: I had killed his wife. My very survival was an affront. And, having survived, I was without any of the child's hold on a parent; for what could he have seen of himself—or of Mother—in me?

"Look at her," Grandmother liked to say, as she pointed her chin at me (as though I was not worth even the effort of raising a finger). "The gargoyle's lucky daughter"—in other words, removed from hideousness by a hair's breadth. Had she called me a gargoyle, it would have been an exaggeration and thus less painful. But it was the precision of her insults that gave them their sting.

My interest in Mother's pictures bordered on idolatry. There was one in particular, an early photograph posed and painted over with a minimum of subtlety, that worked its charm on me. She was sitting with her feet tucked underneath her on a carpet of spiky, artificial grass. A gauzy tunic clung to her thin chest, making it seem almost concave. Her face was tilted back to reveal a smooth stretch of neck, slightly parted lips, and the narrowest of nostrils, while her eyes looked over her shoulder, toward a painted backdrop of coconut palms.

Today I can recall the expression on her face as one of saintly vacuity, like those of the women in holy picture cards. But as a child I saw in that cheap portrait a mother capable of magic and compassion, a mother who, if I stared long enough and begged hard enough, might be moved to work a miracle—the miracle of transferring her own image onto me.

At that age, I felt not just plain but plug-ugly. In a magazine that Father had brought home one day, the cook's wife saw a picture of an Easter Island head and pointed it out to me: "Look, child, look! When did they take this picture of you?" That was my profile; even I could see it. My dark and downtrodden look showed more of an affinity with those stone heads than with my fine-featured mother's.

Whatever his reasons, it was as though Father had failed from the very start to make any connection between himself and me, as though I were someone else's child—deserving of care, yes, but someone else's care. I was well tended by relatives and servants; I wanted for nothing; I was the envy even of less well-off children whose fathers couldn't afford to have them chauffeured to school in outsize limos, who hadn't the means to acquire imported toys and clothes, who could only come home from work each evening and do the ordinary things fathers do: help them with homework, take them for walks or a swim on a summer day.

But as I grew older and every effort, every scheme, every hope of winning him over seemed so unavailing, it couldn't escape me that it wasn't hatred or spite that kept him away. It was simple indifference.

When he left home for the last time without so much as a hint of the imminent separation—let alone a goodbye—I, of course, accepted the official version: that his disappearance had to be kept secret, so that in the event of my capture or torture I would be better off if I had nothing to divulge. We thought like that—we had to—in those sinister days.

But I knew, even as my heart grew heavy with concern for his safety, even as the days, weeks, months passed without word from him, what his silence really meant: not a safety measure; not the pain of separation; no, nothing more than indifference.

It came to me, too, that lingering sorrows—mourning for a dead wife, for instance—were not allowed in Father's scheme of feelings. I once heard him speak to a group of English ladies (a charitable organization). To spur them on in their social work, he quoted their own Lord Dufferin: In one's work there should be no room for good intentions. It was an adage by which he himself lived, except that in his own work there was no room for other sentiments besides. I came to the wisdom that when Mother died, she died as it were without a trace, leaving no ghosts—not even me— to trouble his sleep.

Yet I worshiped him. I worshiped the very imprint of oil left by his mouth on his glass at the dinner table. To see his name in the newspapers, to come up against his face on street posters, to hear the timbre of his voice on radio broadcasts, was to break out in shivers of pride.

Once, churning in bed with yellow fever, I nonetheless knew a night of happiness and hope, all because he had come home with a bag of fruit for me.

It was the summer of the worst drought in years. In the dry zone people had died by the hundreds of heat prostration, and in the village squares the monks were praying out loud for rain.

Between sieges of raging fever, I stared out the window and followed the play of sunlight on the wide, papery leaves of the almond tree. I turned to the same dull fantasy again and again: of plucking an almond, setting it on the ground, smashing it open with a heavy stone—then picking through the stringy, moist shell to find the small nut. Over and over this simple operation turned in my head until, exhausted, I would turn to one of my aunts who sat knitting or tatting at the foot of my bed.

"Is today the day I am to die?"

"Hè! What a thing to say. Rotten mouth. Morbid, morbid child."

(*Yes, today must be the day*, I would think then.)

Death did not seem quite so frightful when I imagined it as a chance to be reunited with Mother. Hadn't she gone into hiding for all those years simply to test my mettle and fidelity? Now, satisfied at last that I had proven myself, she would be waiting on the other side of life, smiling and flinging her arms open in welcome. And as I ran to her, tears would stream down her face and she would say: "I am so proud of you. I will never, never leave you again." Then, moved to pity by my plainness, "Come, let's go inside. I'll see that you look just like me."

And as we walked arm in arm, I could smell on her the fragrances I liked: talcum powder, mint, and freshly cooked wild asparagus dipped in peanut oil.

But in the end it was Father who broke the persistent fever and revived me with his bag of fruit. Even though I was incapable of keeping down anything more than a sip of plain tea or a sliver of ice, I felt nourished by the mere sight of that fruit. He had bought them himself—crisp pears and green grapes—not sent them with a messenger, or left them on a table, but actually stopped on his way home to buy them and bring them home to me.

That night, he announced to my exhausted aunts that he would relieve them in their vigil over me. I remember how lightly he slept on the cot across from me, startled, almost frightened each time I leaned over the bed to vomit—and how he kept tapping against the wall a napkin filled with ice cubes to keep me supplied with crushed ice.

I had rarely been so blissful. I still felt the alternating seizures of heat and chills, but on my bedside table was the bowl of fruit he had brought, and across the room was my father himself, actually watching over me, feeling my forehead from time to time with his cool palm, and losing sleep over me. I wished to be sick forever.

No, being his child wasn't without its rewards. The very infrequency of the favors he bestowed made them memorable. There was that night of the light festival when he led me by the hand—I couldn't have been more than ten years old—through the main promenade in the center of town. Colored lights hung from the jacaranda trees and lit up the façades of the office buildings. Afterwards, we walked to an open-air market, where under a tent bright with pressure lamps, I sat like an adult on a shaky wooden stool and ate piping-hot pieces of fried gourd—even washing it down with greasy black tea.

Occasionally, he would bring home a stack of books and papers to me. They came from all over the world, in languages I couldn't even recognize: pamphlets printed on yellowish paper; thick paperbacks with uncut pages; magazines filled with advertisements showing men and women with wide smiles and perfect teeth. Some of those titles still throng in my head, for, though meaningless at the time, they spelled a kind of flattery to which I wasn't accustomed. It was enough that he thought me equal to them.

It was through almost unthinking gestures like these that he opened my eyes to a world larger than the one immediately within view. I began to sense that life did not begin and end in our small, bypassed land, that I could expect, albeit at some remote point in the future, to strike out in search of what lay beyond—beyond the familiar or the usual.

One morning when the bearer didn't show up, I car-

ried Father's coffee in to him. He was still in bed, seem-
ingly asleep. After setting the tray down on his table, I was
about to leave the room when he stopped me. It was a
school day (I was in elementary school) and I was already
dressed, but in my gym shorts rather than the standard
pinafore.

"Are you doing gymnastics?" he asked.

"Yes," I said, without understanding the word. I could
lie so easily, almost instinctively, for him—out of confusion
and just the desire to please.

"Come and show me." He turned over on his back and
raised his forearms, keeping his elbows propped up on the
bed. "Come stand on my hands." He cupped his palms.

I drew back, full of fear over what I had done.

"Come," he ordered.

I could not disobey him. I climbed up onto the bed,
placed one foot on his palm, found I had nothing to hold
onto, wobbled, and lost my balance.

"Again," he said.

I lifted my foot again and set it down on one of his
hands, which was harder and steadier than I had thought.
He hoisted my other foot before I could waver, so that I was
suddenly standing erect on both his hands, quivering with
relief. Then, his fingers clamped over my feet in a tight grip,
he started to straighten out his arms, and I realized that he
was not going to stop until he had raised me to arm's length.
I began to list wildly, from one side to the other.

"Hold still," he commanded.

Then he did something wholly out of character. He
began to hum a tune. It was a familiar, circusy melody—the
accompaniment to a high-wire act that toured the country
each year. And all of a sudden I realized that I had lost my
fear. I was standing rigid, my legs stiff and stable, Father's
arms equally rigid beneath them. I gazed straight out the
window, from a height I had never seen, over the top of the

pergola that ran from Father's room toward the fruit orchard.

There was nothing extraordinary about the view: the stretch of wisteria vines across the arbor, the tamarind trees with their feathery leaves and hanging pods beyond.

But to this day the memory unfolds before my eyes: the green of the small wisteria leaves (dark in the shade, transparent in the sunlight); the lavender of the blossoms; the pale, patchy sky—and the way a sudden hefty gust of wind shook down a cluster of tamarind pods and set the wisteria leaves trembling as I balanced on my father's hands.

11

Those last few years of Shan's life turned me into a creature caught in the amber of the present. The past provided neither comfort nor sustenance; and what meaning could a future have that held no promise? When I allowed myself to dredge up memories of our previous life, I felt irreparably cut off from all that had gone before: from the names and faces and happenings of my childhood. As escapees from an imprisoned land, my brother and I had lost the right to send and receive mail; and most of the infrequent news from home was bad: fear, privation, arrests, confiscations, deaths, despair.

Exiled from the past, I faced a future without welcome and knew no aspirations beyond the sheer effort it took to propel me through the weight of each heavy day. Because I could envision no purpose worth striving for, I took refuge in mindless, self-forgetful tasks. I learned to saddle myself with a thousand little obligations that helped insulate me from the larger doubts and worries. I tidied and dusted our small apartment as zealously as if accountable for every surface from ceiling to floor. It became a compulsion to ensure that the beds were made, the windows cleaned, and the cutlery drawer properly sorted: the forks in the fork compartment, the spoons with the spoons, the knives with the knives. Grease was not allowed to remain in the oven; dust was not given enough time to settle, even in the hidden corners of the rooms. I spent an entire week chipping off paint—countless coats of old paint—from the network of pipes that ran through my little closet of a bathroom. Asked why, my ready answer would have been: to expose the nice copper pipes that lay under the paint. But that wasn't, of course, the real reason. In truth I cared nothing for copper pipes. I simply needed such deadening obsessions. In the same way, it was easy to fill thick notebooks—as I did—with interminable lists of unnecessary chores. In my life of counterfeit sense and order, I took pride in the fact that I was never late for work, never missed a bus, and never ran out of salt and pepper.

I withdrew in effect to the back of a thick one-way mirror where, believing myself to be of a piece with the observable world, I mimicked its populace and followed its ways, when all the time I was sealed off, unseen and unheard, in solitary confinement of my own making.

My brother's death brought relief such as I hadn't known since Grandmother died and freed us from her daily oppression. In the earlier stages of his breakdown, I had prayed for the miracle that would allow me to wake up one day to the discovery that it had all been a long and cruel dream. But when things got worse and robbed me of optimism, I dreamed wishfully of a catastrophic accident that would put him out of his misery. To have my darkest dream come true, then—to see him die so suddenly, so magically, in the wake of these dreams—was to feel an odd thrill over my own power. For most of my life I had felt small and lacking in the force of will to make things happen. Now, for a change, I could marvel at a miracle that I myself had wrought, simply by wishing. I had merely to wish for a death to have it take place. The wonder of it made me almost euphoric and, in a strange way, incapable of grief.

But it was only a matter of time before the truth caught up with me. Waking at odd hours of increasingly restless nights, I seemed doomed to review, again and again, a starkly incriminating strip of film that had recorded the day of Shan's death. The sequence of scenes would go by like an old familiar movie, but each time the hidden projector would break down and freeze the same frame: the frame that captured me hiding in my room as Shan lay dying in the next.

I saw myself praying, as I had that day—the kind of prayer that speaks not to God, but to one's own flagging will —saying to myself something like: "If I stay here and see nothing, then nothing is happening. Death is not happening. If I don't see my brother dying, then I am not related to him or to his death."

And then I would feel ill with self-blame: for having wished his death in the first place, then for having absented myself from it; for all I hadn't seen of it, all I hadn't felt; and finally, for having failed to take the place of him who had died.

Sometimes I could even work up an anger toward him —anger for branding me with this perpetual guilt. But with the prospect of the loss of guilt came a loss of any warmth toward his memory, which left me more bereft than ever. In an involved way it was the guilt that kept my goodwill from withering. And I was in danger of withering from the inside out.

No matter how much I had hated it at the time, being a nursemaid had given me purpose. Now, with Shan gone, there was nothing left to devote myself to, no pressing tasks to hide behind. My workaday life coasted on its own momentum, like one of those miniature cars that can move along without mechanism on a track that is canted and banked in the proper way. I had only to set myself in position to be carried along through the cycle of each day.

But things started to change about a year after Shan's death. Life was no longer without direction; at last there was something I could commit myself to.

The change came after the news about Father. It arrived in the form of a letter which I recognized at once as originating in the old country. It was written on pink stationery, the kind sold in the tea-and-cigar shops back home, but the handwriting was unfamiliar:

Child, child!
Our hearts are in pieces. Your father died last week, on the 8th of the month. He had been in good health, which is to say fair health. The life we lead here in this remote and unaided corner of the earth inflicts on the strongest of us all manner of hardship and disease. But your father bore them well—not passively and fearfully like us, but with manly impatience. He cursed. He groaned. He complained. He knew he was brave and didn't need to pretend.

Last week he went down to the river to fish, which he liked to do for relaxation when heavy rains restricted our movements. Imagine if you can our days in this jungle. We rise early. We train. We hunt and fish for our food. Often we go hungry. Occasionally, we go to war. This is the rebel's life: a dog's life, really, long periods of waiting, not enough food to eat, and a game of checkers with old bottle caps to break up the long afternoons.

He was gone only for a few minutes and returned to camp without having fished at all, looking very tired. We made him lie down, which seemed to cause pain. He said he felt a severe kind of heartburn. We had eaten venison the night before—some of our men had been lucky in their hunting—and we thought he was suffering from indigestion. That night of his discomfort he ate nothing, and lay very still. His face was the color of powdered lime, but he insisted the pain had passed. Thinking it was nothing serious, we left him as usual to sleep alone in his hut. The next morning, God forgive us, we found him dead.

He wanted to be buried without ceremony, he told us once. We respected his wish, leaving him in the graveyard to lie side by side with the others that gave their lives for our cause, many of whom would have found the nearness to him a privilege and a solace.

No eulogy could detail his sacrifices and achievements. To say that he gave up home and family and riches is to tell only part of the story. A thousand other deeds will hold us forever in his debt. But mainly he gave us the benefit of his rage. It was his terrible anger that shocked us out of our deep sleep of submission and resignation. He reminded us who we were and what we owed to ourselves.

We hope this letter reaches you before too long a delay, since your exact whereabouts are unknown. You have doubtless felt sad over the loss of contact with your father. But it was his way of ensuring your safety, comfort, and success. He felt you were destined for success. He talked of you often, with fondness and pride.

Once, when we were speaking of our children and wondering how different their lives might have been had we remained quiet, accepting men, someone asked your father whether he didn't fear for a daughter who, from a life of security and comfort, was suddenly forced to fend for herself in a strange country. (By then, he had heard of your dear brother's death which hit him hard, poor man, poor father. Poor son!) He said, "She is like me. Not marrow, but iron in her bones."

Pardon us for accepting your father's great sacrifice.

Accept in return, if you will, our blessings for a life that will be easier than the one your father chose on our behalf.

It was signed by one of Father's aides de camp.

I didn't grieve for Father, just as I hadn't grieved for Shan—at least not in the ordinary human way. Denial had become a way of life; it worked as a filter, diluting the strength of all compromising emotions: love, hate, anger, fear, grief. Again, as after Shan's death, I thought I felt relief. I thought I felt free—free from the buffetings of Father's life, from the rumors and sketchy news since his disappearance and our flight from home.

It was this reality, this finality, that conferred upon me a new calling.

One by one my family had died; and I, the survivor, uncovered an identity I had never known. I could see now that I'd been born with the imprint: I had come into the world with a death (my mother's) on my hands, and it seemed increasingly a duty—a family obligation almost—to leave the world in the same way.

Once I could acknowledge this vocation, it was only a short step to plotting my own end.

Under the blows of the past several years I had burrowed into the worst sort of complacency—worst because it was entirely fictitious. There was nothing satisfying about the slavishness of the days, the emptiness of the nights, yet I believed myself satisfied. There were no sustaining friendships to offer comfort, because all my losses had deadened me to the possibilities of friendship.

I was in the grips of a great fatigue—the fatigue of despair—and to step out or reach out in the direction of hope posed an effort of will that seemed far beyond my strength.

Father's death brought a sense of mission that changed all that. Suddenly, there was a project to throw myself into

—a project conceived behind the locked doors of a secretly grieving heart. No one knew, or appeared to care, about the threats on my life, sordid and self-imposed as they were. And so no one could deter me from the battle I was doing with myself, from my games of suicide.

It was this that kept me going: this option of taking the law into my own hands. It was this that filled me with energy: to know that I could number my own days, and not simply wait for them to be claimed by some untimely disease or accident of fate. *Myself unto myself.*

We talk about the fear of dying, but this is loose talk, mainly. Most of us live as if we will live forever; the future runs in our blood. It was not so for me. I began to open myself up to an end—a real end, not just the end of a long day or night, but the end of everything I knew and could no longer bear. And it was this vision—or lack of vision— that brought surcease to what could have been endless days, endless despair.

I once dreamed, during this period, that I was lost in the wilds of an aboriginal land, where a witch doctor, angered by some inadvertent wrong I had committed, placed a curse on me. The curse was to live with the burden of a thousand afternoons. It took some time to understand why such a dream should have the quality of a nightmare. It was simply that what was so normal a part of the unthreatened life—a succession of afternoons—was for me the embodiment of doom.

Now that I am remembering and no longer living that unhappy chapter, I make it all sound so deliberate and abstract, as though the decision to take my own life were a product of the mind alone. In truth, my ability to think clearly and calculatingly about death was only the symptom of an ailment that was festering in the pit of my stomach. Or maybe it was my chest. Or my head. Or perhaps in all three.

It wasn't just idle morbidity that led me to lick the cold metal of a toy revolver and extrapolate the taste of a real barrel in my mouth prior to shattering my brains. It wasn't simply the wish for martyrdom that brought on thoughts of setting myself on fire—although I did long for some sort of recognition. I didn't need a public square or a busy street as the site of immolation, but I did imagine bathing myself in kerosene, lying down in bed, and finally lighting the match that would send the flames eating through my fingers, toes, ears, nose—until all that remained of me was a charred sausage on a smoking mattress.

What moved me to these exercises was as much the bodily aches and pains caused by the soul's distress as that distress itself. My limbs had grown heavy with a kind of arthritic weight. I longed to give up all motion entirely and began to fear each day: the activity, but also the inactivity, that awaited me. I could count on a few finite mechanisms that would see me through the start of each morning— brushing my teeth, brewing coffee, then rinsing out my cup —and I was thankful for them. But when the time came to step out the door, when I could no longer put off facing the world—that was when my eyesight would go.

At first the colors of the street would explode into my vision: the painted houses, the gaudy metal of the automobiles, the loud fabrics worn by people who had become extraterrestrial in their obliviousness to me. But within minutes I would notice the change. The colors around me, the very light itself, would fade—the way it darkens suddenly on winter evenings. Then, everywhere I turned, the world was colored gray—not gray exactly, but the chalky lilacs and duns and buffs of barren winter trees.

And as I began to lose my bearings in that suddenly foggy light, it was all I could do to keep from throwing myself at the feet of passing strangers, or collapsing at every street corner, fire hydrant, mailbox, bus stop, or park bench,

and crying out my misery for all to hear. It was all I could
do not to shout out something like, "Won't somebody help
me?" But even in the grip of this crazy impulse, I was
sufficiently in my right mind to anticipate the responses that
such petulance would be likely to bring.

"Help you? How can I help you? You must help yourself."

"Help you? You need real help, professional help."

So back I went to the old game: toying with thoughts
of a gun in my mouth or fire on my skin. The exercise
brought an almost physical relief. The moment I imagined
the taste of cold metal, or reminded myself of the smell of
kerosene, I could feel a soothing change, like the effect of
milk on an acid stomach. And, taking these fantasies to their
logical end—imagining my head blown apart and spattering
the walls; wondering where in relation to my body the
gun would end up; anticipating the speed of the fire that
would devour me—gave me in a twisted way the strength
to carry on.

Yet there were moments of sobriety when I could see
through myself, when I was forced to admit the simple and
infantile nature of these secret histrionics. I didn't want to
die quietly and unobtrusively: poisons or pills would have
done the job. I wanted to die in such a way as to create a
stir, to make a statement or a splash. I wanted to be discovered in a shocking way, to have someone, anyone, walk into
the scene of the crime and recoil in horror: *Oh, my God!* I
could feel the child in me crying out for attention, crying
out in self-pity, as after some harsh punishment. Even my
motives didn't seem so far removed from the stories children
write when they imagine their death: stories such as, "Once
upon a time I died. My mother came in and cried. Then my
father came in and cried. Everyone was so sad, even the
birds."

Perhaps that was all I wanted: my mother and father to

cry over me, the birds to stop singing for a moment, the earth to show a little compassion over my small but painful fate.

All the time I was plotting these crimes against myself, I did still have a conscience. There were occasions when I would stand over the sink with a razor blade, scraping it lightly over the underside of my left wrist; placing it like a bridge over the two pulsing veins; seeing in my mind's eye the blood that would gush out—then noticing suddenly that the blade was rusty; wondering whether it would cause infection; being struck by the grim illogic of that thought . . . and finally choking up from the futility of everything: my life, my troubles, my unseemly solutions. Then I had to brace myself against the cold sink and ask, with the heaviest of hearts, *Oh, God, what went wrong? How have I come to this?*

Life had its own allure, and I wasn't immune to its persuasions. I could be standing alone in the cold, waiting for a train, a bus, for instance, and catch a glimpse—the most ephemeral glimpse—of a face that would flood me with every kind of longing: for human contact, the fulfillment of a romance, the salve of a friendly talk. And though my life so far had left me only with a glimmering awareness of what such contact, such fulfillment could bring, I could subsist for days on the hope inspired by that unfamiliar face borne away on that vanished bus or train.

But when the hours passed without the telephone ringing or any mail arriving, when the ticking of the clock only confirmed the cancerous futility of my existence, I would take refuge once again in my sordid little schemes of suicide.

Still, from the contemplation of death to death itself is a great leap; and even though I knew that I was painting myself into a hopeless corner, that nothing could be thought about so intensely without its happening, I might not have made that leap in quite the same way if it hadn't been for Commander Morgan.

It takes the littlest provocation to unleash a pent-up anger; it takes the littlest slight to set off a suicide in the making. Still, it is staggering to reflect that I came close to losing my life over some old codger who was losing his marbles.

Commander Morgan lived in my apartment building, on another floor, and, except for the postal error that kept bringing his pension checks to my mailbox, there would have been no occasion to get beyond the pleasantries we exchanged on the elevator.

I could have gone on simply switching the envelopes from my mailbox to his; but when it looked as though this might continue indefinitely, I went to knock on his door with his latest check in hand.

He was a long time answering, but the light under his door kept me waiting. It seemed a safe time to call: I had come straight home from work; it was still early. But when the door opened a crack, I could tell by his confused blinking that he had been asleep. It occurred to me that there were people like him, holding a job but living alone, for whom the day might end at the office, who came home only to sleep off the rest of the lonely evening—just as I myself would have gladly eliminated the hours after work each day by burying myself in bed, if only sleep came easier to me.

He unlatched the chain on the double lock to let me in. The room was identical in size to mine, but so bare as to seem uninhabited: three chairs that didn't match, a card table, a black-and-white television set turned on without the sound—that was all. A counter top separated the main room from the kitchen, where not much more in the way of household amenities was evident.

There was a three-burner gas range, like the one I had, with a single aluminum pot on it; and, beside the si empty foil pan that held the remains of a frozen pie o sort.

It took a while for my explanation about the checks to sink in—he kept shaking himself to wake up—but when it did, there was no shrugging off his gratitude. He went through a silent eenie-meenie-miney-mo to pick out the most comfortable chair for me. He insisted on my having a drink, which he then had to ransack the kitchen for, even though it was only a glass of water.

The tumbler he handed me had a green-and-gold clover design and a cloudy, sticky film of dust. As I raised it to drink, I saw that the ice cubes were discharging strands of scum into the water. I nursed it in my lap without drinking, but this went unnoticed. Eager and exhaustive as only one who is starved of companionship can be, Commander Morgan launched into his life story.

He had been a naval engineer, a shipbuilder who had seen the industry grow from its pre–World War II slack to the fruition of the *Arizona*, the *Iowa*, the *Massachusetts*. After retirement, he had gone on to a second career that allowed him to put to use the languages he had taken up as a sideline: French, Italian, Russian. That part-time government job had led to an assignment in Vietnam where he found himself translating the transcripts of prisoner-of-war interrogations.

After two years he had come home to enjoy his second retirement. But he could never really retire, of course. He was not that kind of man: a life without work was a life without meaning. Now he had a job as a part-time translator for the American office of a French engineering firm. The French company was good enough to let him have his own office, even though half of his time was spent on free-lance work for the government.

By now the Commander was red in the face. Yet he hadn't been drinking. I figured it was from the sheer intoxication of being listened to. He said, "You're very nice to listen to an old man."

I said, "Not at all."

"Oh, yes, my dear, I am," he said, misunderstanding me. "I'm seventy-nine."

He was waiting for some reassurance that he was young for his years. I couldn't bring myself to oblige him, so I said, "How does it feel to be seventy-nine?"

"It feels just awful," he said, putting on a hang-dog look. "When you're as old as I am, you can never hope to have dinner with a woman as young as you."

It was the kind of challenge not meant to be taken seriously, but I wasn't very balanced in those days. He seemed to me frantically lonely, doomed to early evenings and frozen pies. It was nice, for a change, to step out of my own narrow concerns. So I said, a little too readily, "I would enjoy that. We could try the restaurant at the corner, the one that used to be the cleaners. So we wouldn't have to walk far."

"And why wouldn't we want to walk far?" he said, teasing. "I'm not that old, you know."

But he was old enough to put me in mind of Grandmother who seemed, in retrospect, better preserved than he. She was about his age when she died, but even at her worst —bedridden and stripped of power—her flesh was hard and held some vestigial traces of her youth. Commander Morgan was without any physical reference to his younger days. The process of compression brought about by old age was well underway: when the head sinks into the shoulders, when the waist ends up high on the chest, and when only the skin escapes shrinkage, indeed becomes loose enough to gather by the handful and tie into a knot. He had reached the stage of dewlaps and involuntary rumination.

But there was a twinkle behind his bifocals when he came to call for me the next evening. And a white handkerchief in his coat pocket. He was wearing an olive suit so ancient that it had a shine on. In the dim, recessed light of the elevator I noticed the heavy sprinkle of dandruff on his shoulders, and a large stain on one of his trouser legs.

He crooked his elbow in my direction as we stepped off the elevator, and I took it with a curious mixture of embarrassment and elation.

It had been a long time since I was out with a man other than my brother, and as we stood by the door to the restaurant waiting to be seated, the Commander wheezing faintly beside me, the moisture on my brow and palms brought home to me the fact of my arrested, impoverished life. At twenty-five, the anticipation of spending an evening with a man triple my age was enough to leave me tense and sweaty before the evening had even begun.

So there we were, an unlikely pair, both short of breath by the time we were settled in our seats. He held the menu down around his knees for better visibility and stared at it for so long, snoring, that I thought he had gone to sleep.

"This is a little expensive, isn't it?" he said at last. "But what the dickens, it's only once in a while."

I said, "Commander Morgan, please. It's my treat."

His chin, which had been tilted upward the better to look down through his bifocals at the menu, sank down on his chest to look up at me. It was a questioning look: Was there more to my remark than struck the ear?

All at once I felt the inevitability of a letdown to an evening I had approached with almost feverish anticipation. Once this presentiment had struck, it seemed as if everything that followed was simply confirmation.

Halfway through our meal, he raised his glass to me, saying, "I can't remember when I've enjoyed myself so much!" But he had lost interest. He was answering my questions almost reluctantly, no longer concerned to keep an exchange going. And the few questions he asked me were so repetitious that I gave up trying to sort out whether they betrayed a failing curiosity or a failing memory. He was more absorbed in the bread basket, rummaging through the assorted rolls with sober concentration. I noticed how he peeled the crust off a roll as though it were an orange, then buttered it carefully before chewing it. I noticed the crumbs on his necktie. I noticed that when the waiter came to clear his plate, it held a mound of half-chewed meat. It was my private little revenge to notice these things.

Over coffee, he seemed to recover some of his chattiness, and began a rambling story about a trip he had made to the North Pole. I was having trouble following it and was only half-listening when I caught the phrase "that was when a few of my friends were still alive."

Was he, too, all alone in the world, the last survivor of his kin, like me? I felt such a rush of solidarity that I said, "Perhaps we could do this again?"

He began to stir his coffee very deliberately, shaking his head and not looking at me. I repeated my question, in case he hadn't heard.

"Yes. Yes, that would be nice," he said with such sad condescension that I wished I could retract the gesture. When I called for the check, he placed his palm over it. "It's not allowed," he said, sententiously. "You're a lady, aren't you?" I paid it, nonetheless.

By the time we got up to leave, he was no longer talking. I wanted to suggest a stroll through the neighborhood, if only to end things on a better note, but he seemed so tired that I simply walked alongside him the short block to our building. In the elevator, he pressed the button to my floor. "I'll see you to your place," he said, dutiful even though on his last legs. At my door, he shook my hand. "Thank you so much. Good night."

The next morning, I awoke with a sense of danger and immense helplessness, as though stranded on a fragile scaffolding at the top of a high-rise building, with no visible means of reaching the ground. There was a point when I awoke each morning, a moment as brief as the flare of a sparkler, that allowed me to hope. In that split minute of brightness, I saw the possibility of change and betterment, of a turning point that would place back on track a course of life that had become derailed.

But that Saturday morning following dinner with the Commander, there was no such hope to start me off, and when I sat up to face the day, I did not know how I would survive the next hour, let alone the day.

I got out of bed with the difficulty of a bedridden invalid. Upright, I found that I was still steady on my feet. I hadn't listened to the weather reports, so when I went to the window and drew back the drapes, I was taken aback by the snow that had accumulated during the night and was still falling. The cars along the sidewalks were cloaked and whitewashed into insignificant little mounds; the streets were buried; the sidewalks sprouted odd snow-covered objects: a mailbox, a fire hydrant, a trash can. The altered landscape merely gave shape to my dislocation.

Yet I did get through the morning. I brewed coffee and drank it. I washed out my mug. I toasted a slice of bread and ate it. I toasted another slice but lost my appetite before I even buttered it. I made my bed. Directed by some senseless compulsion, I changed the sheets. When I looked at the clock again, I realized that I had succeeded in filling three hours that I had believed upon waking to be beyond filling and enduring.

The knock on the door came as I was standing over the stove, contemplating cleaning the oven.

I opened it without bothering to look through the peephole.

"Commander Morgan!" I said. "Do come in."

Was there hope of companionship after all?

He stood at the door, shuffling his feet. "No, no thank you," he said. "I can't stay. I just wanted to get something off my chest. It has to be said. I wasn't lying when I said I enjoyed having dinner with you. You're a very intelligent young lady, a good listener, fun to be with. But the last thing I want to do is leave the wrong impression."

"What impression?" I said.

"The impression that I'm ready for a serious relationship," he said. "When a woman buys a man dinner, I can't help thinking that the next step is for her to invite him on a hot weekend. Please don't get me wrong. I like you. But there's just no future in this sort of thing. Do you know? I'm sorry."

And he was down the hall before I could recover.

I shut the door and stood leaning against it, suspended between laughter and tears. In the next minute I could have been doubled up at the farce, chalking it up to my own lonely and desperate situation.

But suddenly, on the verge of laughter, I turned to the window and saw in that familiar, frightful way how the world was being drained of its color, how the snow itself was turning into a mass of dull, sandy sediment that might have been blown in by a desert storm. All at once I knew I had reached the moment I had been putting off, and felt a great lifting of the spirits to acknowledge that there was no turning back.

To be rejected by an incontinent seventy-nine-year-old man is not in itself sufficient reason to kill oneself; but when its hour has come, a suicide occurs at the drop of a hat, a flip of the coin. I had rehearsed this moment enough times in my mind to know what to do. I opened a drawer in the kitchen cabinet and found the Exacto knife that I used for newspaper clippings. I put on my coat and boots, slipped the knife in my pocket, and, taking care not to look back and risk vacillation, walked out the door.

The snow had brought with it a loaded silence. The few people I passed seemed to be talking in hushed tones; the cars moved with quiet caution. I could see the low walls of the park toward which I was heading, but still had several blocks to go. Wading through snow as high as my hips, the thought crossed my mind that I had been carrying the seeds of my end—this particular end that was just around the corner—from earliest childhood. Hadn't I gone to bed every single night with death on my mind, praying not to be taken in my sleep?

The next thing I knew, I had reached the park and was stumbling about, looking for the secluded bench that would give me the protection I needed, when I slipped and fell on my knees. And, as long as I was forced into that position, I thought I might as well pray.

It wasn't the same childhood prayer; in the intervening years I had had something of a change of heart. Instead of warding off sudden death, I was now praying for it, devoutly begging for it. The snow was burning into my knees; I felt a fleeting sympathy with the desert fathers who tormented themselves on the boiling sands.

I got up. It was time. I thought I was resigned. But I suddenly found myself swallowing air as I used to in the heat and, in my panic, fearing asphyxiation. Even so, I managed to cross the few yards to the nearest bench, where, parting the snow with my bare hands, I had the inexplicable delicacy to clear a seat for myself.

I sat down in my coat, pulled my arms out of the sleeves, reached into the pocket for the Exacto knife, and with one swift unfaltering motion opened up a gash on the inside of my left arm.

The spurt of blood ran down my fingers and pocked the snow, leaving small craters around my feet.

I was aghast.

Who had done this to me? Who could have done such a thing? I didn't want to be dead! I had wanted to kill myself, yes. But I had really only wanted to kill that part of myself which was causing so much pain. Having done that, I had wanted only to recover and get on with living. So it now seemed.

I didn't want to be dead! I didn't want to miss sunshine or shadow. I didn't want to take leave of all the unfulfilled longings that remained like aches in my bones: for a monsoon shower, for the smell of a fruit or a flower, even for the taste of salts and acids. Everything I was leaving seemed so sweet suddenly; bitterness itself seemed sweet. I had imagined in my spite that the world would be poorer without me. Now I knew that it was really the other way around: I would be a lot poorer without the world. I dreaded the hole I was facing *and* the hole I was leaving.

I felt a surge of nauseating sadness as I realized how precious my own blood had become. Appalled by the waste, I began at first to try to catch the flow in my right palm, then to stanch it with a dam of cupped fingers over the seeping wound that stretched across the inside of my elbow and was sending shock waves of pain through my arm. But the bright red trickle just kept on moving, ineluctably, until there was nothing to do but wait.

In time—in a very short time—a soothing indifference came over me, and I felt myself lifted onto some dim, distant plane where I could split myself off, quite painlessly, from that awful lonely thing I was watching.

12

The nurse had removed the bandage, exposing the foot-long welt with its fishbone stitches, and had gone off to fetch the heat lamp she had forgotten, when Sarah walked into the room. "Dear God, what a mess!" She held her hand over her mouth and sank onto the bed beside me. After a while, she said, staring at her feet, "Funny thing, you know. After all the things I've done to myself, self-destructive things like burning myself with a cigarette and drinking myself into a stupor, the one thing I could never think of doing is killing myself. I just can't see it. Sometimes I had the feeling my parents wished I'd do just that. They've lost track of my tailspins and nosedives, all the admissions and readmissions into just about every nuthouse in the country. I'll be damned if I'll give them the satisfaction."

From her bed across the room, Helga let out a groan of complaint, thrashing about noisily to let us know that she was trying to sleep. But Sarah kept talking, and at last Helga was forced to lift herself out of bed.

"Ach, is it hard to take a little nap in this place!"

On her way to the bathroom, she had to pass my bed. "Ach, Gott, child!" she said, seeing my arm, "Vot you have done to yourself!" She landed heavily on the other side of the bed, her hand brushing the bowl of licorice that Sarah had temporarily set down on the bedside table. Gluttonous from shock, Helga scooped up a handful of the shiny black squares and began feeding herself in small but incessant doses.

"Helga, don't you have to go to the bathroom?" said Sarah.

"*Ja, ja,* I go." But Helga was settling herself more comfortably on the bed. "I tell you something, child." She turned to me. "Vot you did is terrible, but I can understand. Some things I know. *Das Leben ist schwer*. Life is difficult, who can deny? But for you, death is not the answer. I see from your face the first time you walk into the room.

"There is something, an aura. Everyone has auras. No, but of course they do. Your aura is special: orange and bright yellow. Where you come from, they tell you such things, do they not? Those with Eastern religions know what I am talking about."

She reached out for another handful of licorice. "Did you know that all religions are more or less same? Look: The Bhagavad Gita and the Bible and the Koran are much alike, do you see? There is always a prophet, and there is always a dying god. And God vill expose himself in all religions."

"Expose himself?!" said Sarah, rubbing her hands with lewd interest. "You mean like a flasher?" Then she threw herself back on the bed. "Helga, you really take the cake."

Helga said, "You are a strange girl, Sarah. Mit you it is impossible to tell what will be your mood, good or bad; from one day to the next it's a throw up."

Dr. Friday had asked me, toward the end of our first meeting, why I had wanted to die.

I said: "It's not exactly true. If I had sincerely wished to be dead, I would have found a way, probably, to fulfill that wish. It's just that I came to find my life insupportable."

"Insupportable. Like too heavy a burden? Like what?"

I said, "No, worse. Something that suffocates and hurts at the same time."

"Do you feel it now?"

"What?"

"The suffocation, the pain?"

"Right now? No. Right now I am being a patient."

But it would have been more accurate to say that I was being a guest. It was a stranger who had found me, but it was the hospital that had revived me. To be taken in from the cold, as it were, was to be in debt to a favor that I equated with hospitality. This social duty alone made it unthinkable for me to abuse my surroundings by making another attempt on my life. It was enough to assure my safety, to me at least, at a time when I was still a high-risk patient, when I was denied ground privileges and the right to have in my possession any instrument sharper than a soup spoon.

I had said as much at the pass-and-privilege meetings, when I so longed for a walk on my own. I had in effect given my word that I wouldn't "try anything" as long as I was a patient. I knew that I wouldn't be confined forever—a few months at most—and for that length of time I could wait. But my word didn't carry much weight: once a suicide, always a risk.

I had been slow to overcome the initial doubts brought

on by the sight of Dr. Friday's hefty lumberjack's physique and his big, contented, unsuspecting face. It was only on the day Dorothy arrived on the ward that I saw him a little differently.

Dorothy had been transferred directly from Emergency, where she had been revived from an overdose of painkiller. She came into 3 East refusing to speak to any of the patients, except to make the statement, at Group, that the overdose had been accidental, had been merely an attempt to alleviate her chronic back pain.

That afternoon, she was making her way down the hall, her back arched in pain, when Dr. Friday appeared from the nurses' station and caught up with her. Gently, touching no more than the fabric on her sleeve, he took her elbow. "I'm Dr. Friday. I hope the pain is a little better."

I was standing behind them. He hesitated after the word "hope," as if to be careful about what he hoped; and it seemed to me then that in the modesty of his wish was its sincerity: not that the pain would disappear; just that it would get a little better.

Still, I couldn't help blaming him secretly for my continued imprisonment. It was true I could have signed myself out. But to leave the confines of 3 East without official approval was said to be as risky as taking a vacation in a war-torn land.

Weeks passed in that prison without any sense of salvation. Months passed. Years could pass, I thought, and still find me at the dead end I had come to on the outside. Yet I didn't always want to leave. Some days I saw the justice in my confinement. At other times I earnestly wanted to be open to reform. Nevertheless, the drive for freedom at any cost was so strong that I kept up my protest—though it wasn't until the third month that I felt bold enough to press Dr. Friday.

"I have a question," I said toward the end of a private

session, "and I would like a straight answer. How much longer?"

"How much longer?"

(I thought: He's buying time. I must stand my ground, and maybe he will answer me for a change.)

"How much longer must I be here?" I said.

"What thoughts do you have?"

"I just told you. My thoughts are about how much longer I must be here."

"How do you feel about being here?"

I said, "You are like a Russian."

"A Russian?"

"Asking fundamental questions. Do you believe in God? How do you feel about love? Is the universe good or bad?"

"How do you feel about being here?" he persisted.

(I thought: Is that all they're trained to do? Repeat the patient's question?)

I said, "I feel this is a life sentence for such a petty crime."

He was about to light a cigarette, but seemed to think better of it and set the packet on his lap.

"Are you never afraid of what you did?" he asked.

"I am." I didn't mind conceding that.

"Good," he said. "Because it's a very frightening thing." He lit his cigarette. "We have to stop for now."

But once I had broached the question so openly, I couldn't let it drop. *When? How long?* I kept asking.

I said, "I've worked hard. Surely I deserve an answer?"

He took his time answering. Then he said, "I think we *have* worked hard." (The medical "we," I thought. What had he done, anyway?) "But I think we have a lot more work to do. And when the time comes that a successful end to your stay here is in sight, I think we'll both know it."

"Is it time to stop now?" I asked, suddenly very weary.

He looked at me, not at his watch. "Yes, I know," I said

and mocked him: "What comes to mind? I wonder why you ask?"

"I do wonder why you ask," he said. "Why is it important for you to know when to stop? Don't I always tell you?"

"It's important because it's unfair. I'm to lay all my cards on the table while you sit there with your secret thoughts and divulge nothing, not even what time it is when I ask you."

He continued to look at me without speaking, as if I were the one with the answers. The silence affected me; I imagined I could hear the ticking of his wristwatch along with his breathing, a smoker's heavy bronchial rhythm. Slowly, almost stealthily, as though not wanting to disrupt the silence, he reached into his pocket for a cigarette. I saw at last an opening.

I said, "It's discouraging to see that you're like the rest of us. Your smoking. It's harmful, you know it, yet you can't do without it. It's like that with our crazy compulsions. But somehow you'd think, Physician, heal thyself!"

It seemed to me he stopped in mid-puff, but then he exhaled evenly and said, "It's time to stop now."

But the next week he was smoking a pipe. Did I have some effect, after all? If so, maybe it was also in my power to speed things along toward "a successful end." Maybe it was simply a matter of snatching at my most elusive fantasies as they drifted through the mind like exhaled steam in winter air. So I said, "Should I be bringing up certain subjects I haven't talked about so far?"

"What thoughts do you have?" he said, which was his way of asking what I meant.

He was wearing a checked flannel shirt that hung open over a pullover, and corduroy pants that didn't quite cover the tops of his desert boots. I noticed that the heels were caked with mud, with bits of grass around the soles. The mere sight of these scuffs and stains and traces of the outdoors reminded me so keenly of my deprivation that I was seized with the urge to walk out of the building, to cross the highway that separated it from the green fields and white horses I stared at from the window at the end of the hall, and to soil my shoes with mud and grass as he had done his—so unthinkingly, without any appreciation for the freedom it signified.

I saw myself walking across the wide field, dirt on my shoes and the wind in my face, toward a vaguely familiar man who stood among the horses. He was brushing the mane of one of the stallions with a curry comb, deft and unhurried in his movements, while the other two horses stood by calmly as if waiting their turn.

Drawing nearer, I recognized the man: Dr. Friday. He looked at me without surprise, smiling as if I belonged there out in the open as much as he did, while he continued to groom the horses. Not a word was spoken, but I was so gratified to be in the presence of a man who looked as healthy and able and untroubled as he that I went up to him, I actually had the courage to go up to him, and put out my hand.

And when he looked up at me uncomprehendingly, I said, "Yes, I know; it would be unprofessional to take my hand; but perhaps an exception could be made?"

"What are you thinking?" His question broke the reverie.

"Something forbidden," I said.

"Is it about me?"

The bluntness startled me. "Yes."

"Could you say more about it?"

I was thinking of how to delay the admission that lay ahead when he said, "They are fantasies about me? Could you say more?"

I said, "That would be difficult."

"What would the difficulty be?"

"Well. Quite apart from the fact that I'm not used to

sitting in a bare office across from a man and divulging my fantasies about him, I suppose I'm somewhat afraid."

"What would the danger be?"

"Not so much danger as . . . it seems somehow exploitive," I said, "like a game or a tease."

He looked at me without expression. "I can assure you," he said, "that I'll be quite able to handle anything that is said or done in this office." And he smiled to prove his immunity. I realized that he had misunderstood the nature of my fantasy, had expected something more explicit than the sanitized picture of the two of us among the horses—although I knew the scene was probably charged with all kinds of meanings beyond me for the moment. I saw in him the limitations that had discouraged me all along.

I said, "I would like to stop now."

And because the time was not yet up, I spent the remaining minutes sitting before him in silence, staring at his boots which now seemed outsized, filthy, and brutish.

By the time the fourth month came round with no signs of release, I was ready to sign myself out and brave the consequences.

Dr. Friday said, "There's still work to be done."

I said, "You're keeping me here because I'm unrepentant."

"It sounds like you're still concerned about paying for your actions," he said.

"Isn't that what I'm doing here?"

He said, "Have you forgotten why you're here? You sat in a deserted park and knifed yourself. You lost enough blood to . . . you almost didn't make it. I'd like to do what I can to see you don't harm yourself again."

Underneath my shirt, I felt the wound throbbing and itching.

I said, "Please let me go. I don't belong here." I looked

down at my hands; I didn't trust myself to meet his eyes. But it was too late.

I heard him say, his voice suddenly gentle, "If the tears could speak, what would they be saying?"

I just shook my head. But inwardly, I found some satisfaction in ridiculing him for his kindergarten language: Really! If the tears could speak!

If tears could speak, maybe Paddy wouldn't have needed to keep plying me with his letters, which seemed to get longer by the week. I felt the pull of his silence, his notes, his very illness with all its reminders of Shan's. But he had spent much of his adulthood as a patient, and my own prospects for recovery were too shaky for me to return the confidences. I didn't need any great lucidity to see that we were both deficient in ways that canceled out a future. And anyway, I hadn't come to 3 East to answer mail.

He wrote:

I've tried friendship. It doesn't work. Once, a long time ago, my house was open to marauding friends. Back then I didn't mind a lot of activity at night and constant beer drinking, or walking into the house after work and finding my friends already in the living room. Then one night I was fixing a cup of coffee. It was around midnight, everything was quiet and peaceful, when suddenly two black sedans pulled into my driveway and stopped. I couldn't see them but they sounded as though they must have been black. Then somebody banged on the iron knocker from outside. (This was my parents' house; the doors had knockers in that neighborhood.) The duality I felt when walking to the door—(a) my friends had come from Hell for a visit, and (b) Hell was my house for the night and they wanted in—was never resolved, and I welcomed them like a butler in someone else's house, which of course it was. They reminded me of old nightmares in which demons dressed up as clowns would create chaos. An hour and a quarter passed in the kitchen and my laugh-a-minute friends seemed like one big Cat in the Hat. From time to time someone would whisper, "Just tell us if you want us to leave. Really." Which is something like saying, "Just call the police if we steal anything. We'll understand."

I remember needing to lean against the refrigerator for support, to soothe myself with its electric hum, as I thought: I am beyond understanding; I am too far gone to understand.

It took them a long time to give up on me, and none of them realized that it all began that night when I stopped understanding as a matter of course.

So this is not an appeal for responsorial friendship. However. I had a dream in which you played your usual walk-on role of the mystic who speaks in one-line riddles. It began with me sitting in my room, trying to accept the fact that I was dead. I recalled having been sick, then beginning to recover, feeling optimistic, but then seeing the sudden slacking off of the electrocardiogram to a straight line.

After the initial protest, I began to like the feeling of total numbness in the flesh and my blood sitting still in congealed puddles. I was looking forward to lying in bed and letting go, but there was always something holding me back. First it was the knowledge of many things to attend to and the protest against my status as corpse. I was sitting on my bed talking to Molly Flint, who was on the floor, about my dilemma, when I got up to get something, and, coming back to bed, found a deaf-mute Molly there who would not move. This was a nuisance to me, since I was being drained of my strength by the minute and my movements were becoming the mere twitches of rigor mortis. I said, "Molly, how do you expect me to get back on my bed if you're sitting on it?" And she gave me a Mongoloid grin as if to say, "I'm staying here, anyway."

So I had to climb over her and push her aside, which seemed such a waste of power.

Then I was walking in a garden with you with giant cactuses. You were dressed in white, and making this pronouncement: "A creative mind can go either of two ways—forward or backward." From that point on everything disintegrated. For some reason I had to get something to eat with the Clowns from Hell at the all-night coffee shop on 29th Street.

I ate half of a candy bar and wondered if I would be able to digest it. As we were walking into the parking lot, I noticed that the candy had come to a stop halfway down my throat, so I walked into the woods and tried to make myself vomit. Nothing happened, but I was able to urinate, which I attribute to gravity, and I'm sure that that comes as a tremendous relief to you.

When I came back to the parking lot, policemen were leaping in diagonal directions, taking license plate numbers. I thought, God, I hope I don't have to drive. But someone said, "I guess you'll have to drive." So I drove back to my house, figuring on the way that I had at most two days of strength left in me before the final collapse. It was important to complete all affairs before that point, so that I could die without a complex on a bed, so to speak, and not sprawled out on the floor.

The finality of my exhaustion was refreshing, the hope that soon I could give my defunct body the credit for having done all it could. But the longer the dream lasted, the more things appeared on the horizon to be done and the less possible it seemed that I could complete everything on the strength I had left. I thought, Well, I guess Kitty (my sister) will get my typewriter . . . oh, my God, I've got to make out a will, and that means I'll have to contact a lawyer . . . maybe I should spend time with the family before I go, have a cup of coffee and console them . . . maybe I should just write a short letter . . . how am I going to do all this in two days?

That was the feeling it ended with, the recognition that perhaps I had been tricked or hidden the endless list of minutiae from myself in order to avoid an unpleasant death. Any vestiges of the calm I had been expecting were snatched away when the last minor details multiplied and I realized that dying was going to be as complicated as getting married. I faded away still thinking in my chair, hand wrapped around my mouth, profoundly disturbed.

I never intended to cast you in the role of a fortune cookie who speaks one line after thinking about it for twelve days. I never intended to put you in the Ancient Oriental section of the Wax Museum. So put in a good word for me if I am ever captured by your father—and point out to him that if the law is a secret, how can I be blamed for violating it?

The committee in charge of my send-off had kept its secret well; it was only when I left the nurses' station that I guessed what was afoot. There, the staff had been asked to keep me occupied on the pretext of going over yet more forms necessary to my discharge; and when the nurse who had kept eyeing her wristwatch said abruptly, "That's about all for now," I left the room behind the front desk to find the hallway plastered with cardboard posters bearing large arrows that pointed to the dining room and, underneath, crayoned letters announcing my farewell "fête."

The chairs in the dining room had been set alongside the walls, leaving an open space in the center. Up above, multicolored crepe streamers radiated outward from the ceiling fan. The table had been removed to one end of the room and covered with a paper tablecloth edged with a poinsettia and holly design. The buffet had already been set: chocolate cake, chocolate-chip cookies, potato chips, fruit punch, and ham slices in tiny buns. At one end of the table was a pile of packages, some wrapped in foil, some in tissue paper.

Sarah came up from behind and placed her hands over

my eyes, saying, "Surprise!" When I turned around, everyone was there: Winston in an open-necked shirt revealing a mist of talcum powder; Helga in a flowered dress; Maria clutching an embroidered purse; Letty in peach-colored pants and a silk blouse to match; Robin in a flowing cotton dress with leg o'mutton sleeves; Paddy in a wrinkled Hawaiian shirt; and Sarah looking almost unrecognizably groomed and demure in a long cheesecloth skirt and ruffled blouse.

"Open," she said, pointing to the packages. "This is one of those bass-ackward parties: You get to open the presents first."

Then, imitating an auctioneer at a country fair, she kept up a patter as I unwrapped each package: "Now, folks, have you seen the likes of this beautiful multicolored scarf? An asset to any wardrobe, matches every color in the rainbow, and crocheted by none other than Winston, the Disco King of 3 East . . . and from Paddy, another man of many talents, we have . . . well, would you look at what we have? A pair of gen-you-wine leather moccasins, again handcrafted in our own backyard. I ask you, folks: Would anyone know these beautiful, skin-soft moccasins came in a kit? . . . Moving right along, we have an exquisitely—and I mean exquisitely —hand-embroidered linen handkerchief from Miz Maria . . . and from Miz Jolene comes a treasure, a gem, a book! Not just any old book, no sir, but that all-time best-seller, *The Beaneaters*! Yes, well. We know what happens to them. Beans, beans, the musical fruit . . . Oh my word, do my eyes deceive me? Here we have a bag of homemade, delicious chocolate-chip cookies from the original cookie freak, Frau Helga! That she would part with them, folks, is a sacrifice, a hardship such as we might never again see in our lifetimes. . . . Let's hope she doesn't break down and eat them all at one sitting before we've had a chance to sample her handiwork. . . . And now, last but not least, we have not one, not two, but three, folks, three perfect cardamom loaves donated by that great philanthropist, Sarah! And now . . . to the table!"

Winston had put on a record that filled the room with the thumping, insistent beat of a racing heart. The next minute, he had pulled Sarah to her feet, and the two of them were grinding their hips in concert and laughing in each other's faces. Robin and Helga were waltzing together, arm in arm, intent on their own rhythm. Later, during a game of charades, Robin drew *Hamlet* and won cheers and claps when she ran to the table and came back waving a slice of ham, extracted from one of the buns.

When the punch was down to its dregs and the group had thinned out, I sat down next to one of the night nurses who had just come in with her needlepoint kit. She said, "How do you feel about leaving tomorrow?"

I said, "I'm ready."

She looked at me with raised eyebrows—a look that may simply have been a request for more information, but which came across as one of sheer disbelief, as if I had just announced the intention to cross the Pacific in a balloon. I wanted suddenly to strike her across her smiling, composed face. To control myself, I watched her needle plunge in and out of her half-finished tapestry. At last I said, "How long will you have spent on this when it's done?"

She said, "My husband would say forever. He can't understand all this time that goes into it."

"Is your husband a doctor?" I asked. I was just making conversation.

"You know I'd rather not discuss my private life," she said, suddenly prim and official.

Sarah overheard this exchange and shook her head. "Why do we even bother?" she said to me. "They're not human; they're clones." She got up to leave. "I don't know about the rest of you, but I'm beat." The piece of green yarn that had held her long hair up in a ponytail had slipped down to her shoulders. She pulled it loose and draped it over the nurse's face.

The nurse threw the ribbon at Sarah's back and said, "Grow up, Sarah." There was no affection in her voice.

The next morning, with less than an hour left before the cab would arrive to pick me up, I went in for my last session with Dr. Friday. Time dragged. I could think of little to say. Finally I said, "I don't know what I've accomplished in these four months, but I would like to thank you. You listened."

"Do you have any last thoughts about leaving?"

"No," I said, "nothing to write home about. Maybe I just don't care."

"Could it be you care so much that you will deny it at all costs?"

I said, "I don't think I'm denying anything."

"It seems difficult for you to admit that you will miss me or anyone else here."

"I have nothing against admitting that."

"Perhaps you fear that I, too, will be yet another significant figure in your life to abandon you?"

I said, "A reasonable fear, wouldn't you say?"

The time was almost up, so I said, "I have no farewell gift for you. No woodcut or hand-carved belt from OT. But I wish you well." I stood up and held out my hand. "Goodbye."

He rose out of his chair and shook my hand. "All the best to you," he said. If there was any change in his expression, it was too subtle for me to detect. He opened the door for me. And that was all.

I passed Kim, the social worker, in the hallway. "Think of it," she said. "You're leaving!" Then, offering her own brand of encouragement, "It won't be easy on the outside." As I turned to leave, she threw out one crumb of wisdom: "Remember. Rome wasn't built in a day."

I thought about that for a while—not just the ill-fitting metaphor of Rome, but about the accidental insight in that remark. Kim had hit upon the peculiar logic of a suicide, according to which a serious and dedicated process of building goes into the act of self-destruction. Coming from Kim, any wisdom would have to be inadvertent.

By the time I had signed the last of the discharge forms, Sarah and Winston had carried my things outside and placed them in the backseat of the cab. Winston, formal to the last, stuck out his hand. "It's been a real pleasure."

Sarah clasped me briefly. She wasn't eager to linger. "Hang by your toes, friend. I happen to like you."

Paddy was circling the cab as if thinking of putting a down payment on it. As I got into the backseat, he handed me his notebook—the one in which he had scribbled the lyrics to his songs. I turned it over in my hand before it sunk in that he wanted me to keep it. When I looked up, he was already walking away. I got out of the cab and ran after him. "Paddy. Wait. You haven't said goodbye."

He kept on walking. And when I caught up with him he said, in a calm, perfectly clear and well-modulated voice, "Go to hell. Rub someone's back once and you think you're such a hot shit."

When I was finally out on the road, I leafed through the book. In one of the pages, he had written: "Happiness, too, is inevitable."

13

When I was out on my own again, I saw that the months at 3 East had been little more than a hiatus allowing a suspension of time and responsibility. I felt like an invalid who had been forced into a prolonged bed rest—only to find when it came to an end that the old symptoms were still there after all. Back on the outside, no ready cures awaited me. The part of me that wanted to endure still suffered from the absence of a dream to live by, still failed to imagine a future with any real promise of a healing, much less a flowering of my better self. At twenty-five, despite all that had happened to me, I was aware of my meagerness, of how much there was to me that was unused and unlived.

But though the life I returned to was oddly intact, with the same possibilities to explore and fears to face, there was a difference: an edge to my life now that had come about only because I had tried to end it. That attempt was to cause me shame sometimes—shame at having first failed to live, and then at having failed to die. But in time I saw this as a breakdown of intelligence more than of courage, and today I think of that desperate and brutal act carried out in the park as the bravest thing I have done—not because I who fear pain with a weakling's fear could sit there and subject myself to such searing pain; not because I who can feel my gorge rise at the sight of blood actually, willfully, spilled my own; but because I had done *something* to take command of my broken, untenable life. Incidentally, I had defied death, life's greatest fear, and had lived as it were to tell the tale. This gave me a kind of courage I had never known, a sense of hard-earned adventure such as explorers must feel who return from unmapped regions.

The precedent set by this remarkable act was the source of some comfort whenever I felt the old darkness close around me. Having done it once, it was within my capacity to do it again. It made me wary of myself, of the desperado in me. And if I needed any reminder, I had only to roll up my left sleeve where a darkish surgical seam across the inside of my elbow told me, as Paddy once wrote in a note to me: "Your wound is nature's way of saying, 'Remember that firefight.'"

Something else had changed. At 3 East there had been much talk about keeping the doubts and unknowns at bay by taking each day as it came. But I had been doing that all along —too much of that, in fact—and it was time for me to take a little more of each day into myself, to face the present as squarely as I dared. Then, as I began gradually to shake off the sleepwalker's passivity, it became easier to depend upon the solidity of what was real and immediate—the people on the bus, the book in my hand, the rice on my table, the ache in my shoulders after a hard day's work—and to open myself up by small degrees to the oceanic flood of the past.

In time I came to see my father in a truer field of vision than was possible through the warping lens of a child's unrequited and unquenched love. Once I could rise above my preoccupation with injury suffered at his hands, I could begin to see him as he was: a man with a calling, blessed with charisma but flawed all the same. To cut him down to size without butchering his memory—that was the most I could hope to achieve in the way of balance.

The other adults who were part of the life I had buried began slowly to rise up in me once more. It was too soon for me to want to return home, even if it were possible to do so. (Father's death had changed nothing; his enemies still remained in power.) But even if I could, I was not brave enough to find out for certain the fate of my uncle and aunts, who in my mind had been consigned to death—the natural death that follows hopeless separation.

Bit by bit, however, I could bear to think of them again, to imagine completing the letter one day that I had begun in my head: *Dear Uncle! Dear Auntie Lily! Dear Auntie Rosie! If you believe the saying, "Only rivers and streams can disappear without a trace; people cannot," you will believe that I have not forgotten you.*

Mourning my brother's death was the hardest of all. Sorting through his trunk one day, almost two years after his death, I allowed myself at last to linger over the memorabilia of his troubled last years: a broken dulcimer he had picked up at a church fair and intended to mend; a few books on celestial navigation; some unused camping equipment that included a small gas stove, a set of crampons, and a length of plastic rope—all for the expedition that never materialized. And, in a rusty box of fishing tackle, I found the book he had tried for so many years to get me to read when we were locked in argument over his obsession with the coffin tree.

It had been given to him, he said, by the old opium eater in Chinatown. Shan had held on to it as a charm, as a blueprint for the prosperity that would be his one day, when he could return to coffinwood country to take up the old man's trail. He talked about returning to our country and proceeding to the Northern Frontier, where with the help of coolies he would breathe life back into the industry. And even when he had given up trying to enlist me, the unbeliever, I remembered many hours when he was lost in this book.

It was written in the curlicued script of our classical language, on a long sheet of parchment—a reproduction of the books of olden days. The parchment was folded into accordion pleats, each fold marking a page, and bound on either end with a "cover" of bamboo and a tassel of black string that held the folds together when the book was closed. When we were growing up and the country was still open to tourism, the shops along the bridges leading to our temples were full of these bogus documents of no particular literary or historic value, but for which the tourists were ready anyway to pay through their noses.

Now, with the strings untied and the long sheet spread out on the floor, I read the book for the first time from beginning to end. The book told a legend: of a spirit in the coffin tree:

> *. . . A spirit that knows*
> *The after-death secrets.*
> *It will guide your suffering soul*
> *Through the shadow world,*
> *The world between death and resurrection.*
>
> *When you, the know-nothing,*
> *Arrive at death's door*
> *Empty-handed, thick-headed,*
> *The Spirit will give you*
> *The courage to surrender*
> *To the black phantoms waiting.*
> *There are many. Many and many.*

Death is like this:
The body sinks
As if into water,
Clammy and cold at first,
But slowly eaten by flames,
Then blown into a thousand pieces
And scattered through the air.

You will hear
The roll of distant drums;
The clash of cymbals;
A wind soughing
Through tree-branch and sea-shell;
The faint ringing of bells;
A soft humming;
A tapping and wailing;
And the shrill moan
Of a mouth blowing
Through human bone.

You will see the offerings of your kin:
The clothes they have stripped off you,
The place they have swept for you.
Unaware of your own death,
You will call to them;
But they, in tears,
Will be deaf to your words,
And you in your misery
Will go your lonely way.

On you will go, poor mortal,
As you must.
There is no rest for the dead.
On you will go
Past home and kin,
Past your old self.
Then, heavy of heart,
You will say to yourself:

"Oh, I am dead. What shall I do?
Would that I had
My old body again!"

But your body by then
Will lie freezing in winter snow,
Or rotting in summer steam,
Or burning on the family pyres,
Or buried in the ground,
Or covered in water,
Or flung to the birds and beasts of prey.

Now come the shapes and sounds and lights
To dazzle you.
Now come the colors of the elements,
As clear and as finely spun
As the rays of the sun.
Now comes the Spirit to say:
"Fear not. These are the
Shapes, sounds, lights, and colors
Of your own true radiance."

And when you hear the echoes
Of a thousand thunders
Ringing with cries to kill, kill, kill,
The Spirit will say:
"These are nothing more
Than the truth of your innermost self."

So, too, with the gods of death
Bound to visit you:
Those gods with the appetites
Of grave-yard gluttons,
Who fall upon their prey
Like wild cadavers:
Tearing off a head here,
Plucking out a heart there,

Sucking through their long teeth,
Glassy-eyed and pot-bellied
From their human feast.

The Spirit will reveal then
A truth hard to believe:
That these repellent gods
With their eyes aglow,
Their teeth a-chatter,
And blood on their chins
Are nothing but the phantoms
Imprisoned in your soul.

And though a wicked wind
Will whip you from behind;
Though darkness will fall
And the night become shrill
With those angry orders
To kill, kill, kill;
Though hacked to pieces
And racked with pain,
Your body will come together again.

Now comes the Spirit to remind you again
Not to be distracted,
Not to wander about
Like a feather in a gale;
But to prepare for the moment
To be born again.

Now visions of your new birth place
Will shine upon you,
Staining your skin
With the color of the future.
Now the Spirit will lead you
To the home you choose.

You will see the mating
Of men and women;
You will feel the storm of raucous rain.

This will be the moment
You could be born
A horse, a fowl, a dog, or a man.
Hold fast, Dead One,
Hold fast.
Your life-cycle is about to begin.

And give thanks to the Spirit
Of the Coffin Tree.

Exactly what it was about this book that captivated my brother I would never know; but now I thought of the proverb, "The secrets of another are deep enough to drown in."

I knew that Shan had kept many dreams from me, not wanting to subject them, perhaps, to my doubting, scoffing ways. And believing his fantasies to be simple-minded, I had never probed too deeply. It was all part of that old collusion. Something about the way we pitted ourselves against The Others—first as children, and later as wary immigrants—had required a mutual acceptance which if it wasn't exactly blind was as good as dumb.

I thought I had figured out all the important things: how his fabrications reflected an excess of imagination coupled with an excess of fear; how he needed to construct a world catastrophic enough to accommodate these overblown fears; how it was easier for him, for all these reasons, to live in the future.

But I had missed so much else! So many deeper and trickier contradictions! What was the real nature of his interest in the coffin tree? I had assumed it was the belief that it would make him rich. Toward the end of Shan's life, I had come to regard him as a creature degraded into an existence of cunning and shallow wants, like that of a crow, with one eye on the lookout for danger, the other on the prowl for shiny things.

This view had blinded me to a stranger truth. All along I had taken the book on the coffin tree to be a piece of chicanery, a fake map leading to a bogus treasure. Instead, I discovered a legend of other-worldly concerns—so remote from what I had thought Shan's to be.

I could not divine the promise held out by this legend, but I suspected it helped him flee the persecutions of the moment and gave him a story to calm his terrors. It was more than I'd had.

Here was the bane of my discovery: I had pitied Shan for being a cripple, but on his own he had found a crutch —while I, once able-bodied but now disabled, had nothing as yet to lean on.

If I accepted the world, it was this rootless, chaotic world I inhabited and knew; no other. If I believed in life, it was not life after death, but *this* life; nothing less, nothing more.

Yet it was clearer to me now that just to continue in this immediate world, this terminal life, I needed my own version of the coffin tree—some story to tell myself, some illusion to shape the future, some dream to lighten the days.

But maybe the only dreams I would have were the ones in my sleep, when "that old fool, the unconscious," went wandering through the country of the past.

Up until Shan's death, my dreams were frequent and vividly recalled. But after he died I seemed to stop dreaming —or at least remembering my dreams. There were two clear exceptions, however: once when I saw the glass figures after I had been rescued in the park; and then, a year later, on the night I first read Shan's book on the coffin tree.

In my dream, I was back in monsoon country, making a journey to the north, where I knew something important awaited me. From the window of the smooth, buoyant train that was carrying me up through the mountains, I passed tiers of glinting rice fields that became smaller and smaller as I gained altitude, until they turned into tiny green steps in a dwarf land before disappearing altogether.

The train crossed a bridge that spanned an abysmal gully along the sides of which bloomed sprinklings of edelweiss. When I looked back at the bridge we had just crossed, I saw a mountain woman clambering across it, swinging on the underside of the trestles like an ape. Strapped into a pouch on her back was a baby, unperturbed and shaking a rattle.

Then I caught sight of a hairy mountain man—or at least he seemed covered with hair until I realized that he was clothed in bear skins. He was eating something out of a banana leaf, but before I could get a better look at him, he disappeared into a cave. Higher up in our tracks I saw him again: He seemed to be stumbling over rocks and roots, slipping on the ground and hurrying along.

The train had climbed into cold, cloudy regions where the mountain peaks would move out of the mist briefly to expose their ice-blue spires and towers, then retreat once more into the milky sky.

The train stopped at a small station. There, on the pavement, was the mountain man again, huddled over a meal of tree bark that was crawling with white ants. As I watched, I realized that the white ants were actually maggots and I cried out to warn the man. He looked up at me, startled. I saw his face for the first time: Shan.

Just at that moment the train pulled out of the station. I was annoyed to see that instead of running after me, my brother merely got up and walked away in the opposite direction. He had shed his animal skins, and his back was striped with scars and welts.

I was in crisp alpine country now: the fields grassy and covered with spring blossoms, the rhododendron bushes in full flower, the smell of honeysuckle in the air—and bands of monkeys sailing through the tall pines. I could feel the train braking, though there was no station in sight. When it had come to a full stop I got out and looked around, still wondering where I was.

I heard something like a waterfall in the distance, and began to walk toward the sound, stopping to touch the strange orchids that appeared on the shrubs along the way. The sound of water grew louder and louder; I knew I was getting close.

At last I saw what it was: not a waterfall, but a noisy, churning, roiling pool of water where a river was splitting in two. There, at the juncture of the two diverging streams, stood a massive tree. It was a rust-colored pillar that towered to an awesome height, and was crowned by a graceful pagoda of leaves.

I stood aghast at my good fortune: This had to be the rare coffin tree! I took a few steps closer to get a better look at the leaves so high above. This time I saw something suspended from the branches. I craned my neck and strained my eyes. And suddenly I could make it out: the body of a man, encased in ice, hanging from the top of the tree. I didn't need to get any closer to see that it was my brother.

"That poor man," said a voice beside me. I turned and faced a stranger. How had I escaped noticing him before? He was wearing thick boots and was laden with all sorts of ropes and hooks that identified him as a mountain climber.

"It isn't so bad," I said, trying to seem calm in the face of the terrible fear that had seized me. "He seems at peace. All his life he meant to find the coffin tree. Now he's found it."

The mountain climber looked at me with open contempt. "What kind of a being are you?" he said. "Where is your heart? Where is simple human compassion?"

I felt my eyes brimming over at the injustice of his judgment; but before I could defend myself, he said, "Anyway, you're wrong about that tree. That's not a coffin tree.

That's a juniper, often mistaken for the coffin tree, but . . . here, I'll show you." And he began to thumb through a book illustrated with leaves and trees.

But there was no reason for me to stay. "He was mistaken, then," I said as I walked away, brushing off the rain that was drenching my face.

I woke up to desolation that threatened to break my heart, my will, my very soul. But when I had touched my damp pillow and collected my thoughts, the astounding thing to me was that I *had* woken up, that I *was* still alive, even after that dreadful revelation—actually sitting up in bed, wiping away the tears, shivering, remembering. There I was, devastated by a dream which was more than a dream; lonely and unhappy, yet unable to hide from myself; but still stubbornly among the living.

Many more years were to pass before I could sit at my table for an hour or two each night and labor over these pages. But when I was ready, it was this truth that offered itself as a beginning:

Living things prefer to go on living.

A NOTE ABOUT THE AUTHOR

Wendy Law-Yone was born in Mandalay, Burma, and lived in Rangoon until she was twenty. A life-long student of languages, she has been a free-lance writer and editor since 1968. Ms. Law-Yone is married, the mother of three children, and lives in Washington, D.C. *The Coffin Tree* is her first novel.